TOM CORBETT, SPACE CADET:

TREACHERY IN OUTER SPACE

A NOVEL BY
CAREY ROCKWELL

WILLY LEY
TECHNICAL ADVISOR

R🜨CKET SCIENCE BOOKS
AN IMPRINT OF DEAD LETTER PRESS
WWW.DEADLETTERPRESS.COM

TOM CORBETT, SPACE CADET:
TREACHERY IN OUTER SPACE

Published 2018 by
ROCKET SCIENCE BOOKS
An imprint of
DEAD LETTER PRESS
WWW.DEADLETTERPRESS.COM
BOX 134, NEW KENT, VIRGINIA 23124-0134

Originally published in 1954 by Grosset & Dunlap, New York; and by permission of Rockhill Radio. This edition is © 2018 by Tom English.

Cover illustration by Ed Valigursky and the Rocket Science Engineering Department; original interior illustrations by Louis Glanzman. Introduction © Series Editor Tom English.

Printed in the United States of America

ISBN-10: 1-7324344-0-9
ISBN-13: 978-1-7324344-0-0

FIRST ROCKET SCIENCE EDITION: June 2018

THE WAY
THINGS SHOULD BE!

IN 1954, THE YEAR *Treachery in Outer Space* was first published, change was in the air.

Abroad, the First Indo-China War came to an end, with France withdrawing its troops from Vietnam. Following the Geneva Conference, in July, the country was split along the 17th parallel, dividing the Communist-controlled North from the Western-controlled South, and setting the stage for United States involvement in the Vietnam War.

In the United Kingdom, Great Britain finally ended its wartime rationing; and Roger Bannister broke the 4-minute mile. Bannister's record-setting time of 3 minutes 59.4 seconds was cheered by 3,000 spectators at Iffley Road track in Oxford, in a race televised live by the BBC with commentary by 1924 Olympic Gold-Medalist Harold Abrahams —the subject of the 1981 movie *Chariots of Fire.*

In Morocco, a swarm of desert locusts managed to destroy $14 million dollars in citrus fruit in just six weeks. And in the South Pacific, on Bikini Atoll, the U.S. detonated the first hydrogen bomb, which managed to contaminate the fishing vessel *The Lucky Dragon*—operating 80 miles from the test area, and 14 miles outside the designated Danger Area—with nuclear fallout. For three hours a sticky white *shi no hai* (death ash) fell upon the crew of 23 Japanese fishermen, ultimately resulting in the death of one, and severe radiation sickness for the others. Additionally, the Japanese fishing industry lost millions of dollars over the next several years, due to contaminated seafood. The tragedy provided the inspiration for the 1954 Toho film *Godzilla.* (Seriously, you *have* to watch the original version in Japanese.)

At home in the U.S., the Supreme Court ruled that segregation in public schools was unconstitutional, and any state-mandated "separate but equal" policies would no longer be tolerated. The decision helped advance the Civil Rights Movement in America. Also, Senator Joseph McCarthy's "Red Scare" Communist witch hunt effectively came to an end when McCarthy was formally censured by the U.S. Senate in November of 1954. This public censure came only a few months after TV audiences watched McCarthy "self destruct" during televised hearings.

Perhaps on a more comforting note, the mass vaccination of children against polio began, signaling victory over the crippling disease; U.S. scientists invented the solar cell; J.R.R. Tolkien published the first of his Lord of the Rings novels; RCA marketed the first color television sets, and Swanson started selling TV dinners.

And if this were not enough, Elvis Presley recorded his first commercial record (—and yes, friends, it was on vinyl); Bill Haley and the Comets encouraged teenagers to "Rock Around the Clock"; and Americans dived into a new trend for home repair and maintenance: Do It Yourself!

Yes, great change was in the air. And yet, at least one thing remained constant in 1954: the Tom Corbett, Space Cadet novels. Readers could always count on Tom and his pals Roger Manning and the big Venusian Astro to lead them on hair-raising adventures in outer space—and more importantly, to always do the *right* thing at the *right* time.

A good thing indeed, this latter quality of the cadets, because throughout the eight Corbett books, the famed *Polaris* unit demonstrate again and again their amazing talent for being in the *wrong* place at the *wrong* time. Such is the case in *Treachery in Outer Space,* the sixth installment in the series.

So, no matter where danger and duty take them—whether Tom, Roger and Astro stumble upon another sinister plot to overthrow the Solar Alliance, or once again run afoul of conniving bureaucrats or madmen bent on revenge—we can trust the famed *Polaris* crew not only to prevail, but to do so with honor and integrity. In the words of their commanding officer, Captain Steve Strong, "These are special types we train to take care of space rats!"

Good guys winning ... in good old-fashioned adventures. Isn't that the way things should be? May it never change.

Tom English
New Kent, VA

Tom Corbett, Space Cadet blasted across the airwaves in 1950, when CBS debuted the Rockhill Studios television series. The show ran for five seasons, during which it appeared on all four networks of the day. It also launched a successful newspaper strip, a radio show (as *Space Cadet*), and a series of Dell comic books, not to mention scores of LP records, lunch boxes, toys, promotional giveaways, and eight science fiction novels by Carey Rockwell (with an assist from rocketry expert and space-flight advocate Willy Ley, who served as Technical Advisor to both the books and the television show).

THE **TOM CORBETT, SPACE CADET** SERIES

NOW AVAILABLE FROM ROCKET SCIENCE BOOKS:

> *STAND BY FOR MARS!*
> *DANGER IN DEEP SPACE*
> *ON THE TRAIL OF THE SPACE PIRATES*
> *THE SPACE PIONEERS*
> *THE REVOLT ON VENUS*
> *TREACHERY IN OUTER SPACE*

FORTHCOMING FROM ROCKET SCIENCE BOOKS:

> *SABOTAGE IN SPACE*
> *THE ROBOT ROCKET*

TOM CORBETT, SPACE CADET:
TREACHERY IN OUTER SPACE

1 **"ALL RIGHT, YOU BLASTED EARTHWORMS! *STAND TO!*"**
Three frightened cadet candidates for Space Academy
stiffened their backs and stood at rigid attention as
Astro faced them, a furious scowl on his rugged features.
Behind him, Tom Corbett and Roger Manning lounged on
the dormitory bunks, watching their unit mate blast the

freshman cadets and trying to keep from laughing. It wasn't long ago that they had gone through the terrifying experience of being hazed by stern upperclassmen and they knew how the three pink-cheeked boys in front of them felt.

"So," bawled Astro, "you want to blast off, do you?"

Neither of the three boys answered.

"Speak when you're spoken to, Mister!" snapped Roger at the boy in the middle.

"Answer the question!" barked Tom, finding it difficult to maintain his role of stern disciplinarian.

"Y-y-yes, sir," finally came a mumbled reply.

"What's your name? And don't say 'sir' to me!" roared Astro.

"Coglin, sir," gulped the boy.

"Don't say 'SIR'!"

"Yes, sir—er—I mean, OK," stuttered Coglin.

"And don't say OK, either," Roger chimed in.

"Yes ... all right ... fine." The boy's face was flushed with desperation.

Astro stepped forward, his chin jutting out. "For your information," he bawled, "the correct manner of address is 'Very well.'"

"Very well," stammered Coglin.

Astro shook his head and turned back to Tom and Roger. "Have you ever seen a greater display of audacity and sheer gall?" he demanded. "The nerve of these three infants assuming that they could ever become Space Cadets!"

Tom and Roger laughed, not at the three Earthworms, but at Astro's sudden eloquence. The giant Venusian cadet usually limited his comments to a gruff Yes or No, or at most, a garbled sentence full of a veteran spaceman's oaths. Then, resuming his stern expression, Roger faced the three boys.

"Sound off! Quick!" he demanded.

"Coglin, John."

"Spears, Albert."

"Duke, Phineas."

"You call those *names*?" Roger snorted incredulously. "Which of you ground crawlers is radar officer?"

"I am, very well," replied Spears.

The blond-haired cadet stared at him in amazement.

"Very well, what?" he demanded.

"You said that's the correct form of address," replied Spears doggedly.

Roger turned to Tom. "Well, thump my rockets," he exclaimed, "I didn't know they made them that dumb any more!"

"Who is the command cadet?" asked Tom, suppressing a grin.

"I am, very well," replied Duke.

"How fast is fast?"

"Fast is as fast must be, without being either supersonic or turgid. Fast is necessarily that amount of speed that will not be the most nor the least, yet will be sufficient unto the demands of fast..." Duke quoted directly from the *Earthworm Manual*, a book that was not prescribed learning in the Academy, but woe unto the Earthworm who did not know it by heart when questioned by a cadet upperclassman.

"What is a blip on a radar, Mister?" demanded Roger of Spears.

"A blip is never a slip. It is constant with the eye of the beholder, and constant with the constant that is always—" Spears faltered, his face flushing with embarrassment.

"Always what?" hounded Roger.

"I—I don't know," stammered the fledgling helplessly.

"*You don't know?*" yelled Roger. He looked at Tom and Astro, shaking his head. "He doesn't know." The two cadets frowned at the quivering boy and Roger faced him again. "For your information, Mr. Spears," he said at his sarcastic best, "there are five words remaining in that sentence. And for each word, you will spend one hour cleaning this room. Is that clear?"

Spears could only nod his head.

"And for your further information," continued Roger, "the remaining words are 'constantly alert to constant dangers'! Does that help you, Mister?"

"Yes, Cadet Manning," gulped Spears. "You are very kind to give me this information. And it will be a great honor to clean your room."

Astro stepped forward to take his turn. He towered over

the remaining cadet candidate and glowered at the thoroughly frightened boy. "So," he roared, "I guess this means you're going to handle the power deck in one of our space buckets, eh?"

"Yes, very well," came the quavering, high-pitched reply.

"Give me the correction of thrust when you are underway in a forward motion and you receive orders from the control deck for immediate reversal."

Coglin closed his eyes, took a deep breath, and the words poured from his lips. "To go forward is to overtake space, and to go sternward is to retake space already overtaken. To correct thrust, I would figure in the beginning of my flight how much space I intended to take and how much I would retake, and since overtake and retake are both additional quotients that have not been divided, I will add them together and arrive at a correction." The cadet candidate stopped abruptly, gasping for breath.

Secretly disappointed at the accuracy of the reply, Astro grunted and turned to Tom and Roger. "Any questions before they blast off on their solo hop?" he growled.

The two cadets shook their heads and Roger quickly lined three chairs in a row. Tom addressed the frightened boys solemnly. "This is your spaceship. The first chair is the command deck; second, radar deck; third, power deck. Take your stations and stand by to blast off."

Spears, Coglin, and Duke jumped into the chairs and Tom walked around them eying them coldly. "Now, Misters," he said, "you are to blast off, make a complete circle of the Earth, and return to the Academy spaceport for a touchdown. Is that clearly understood?"

"All clear," chorused the boys.

"Stand by to raise ship!" bawled Tom.

"Power deck, check in!" snapped Duke from the first chair. "Radar deck, check in!"

"Just one moment, Mister," interrupted Roger. "When you issue an order over the intercom, I want to see you pick up that mike. I want to see all the motions. It's up to you, Misters, to make us believe that you are blasting off!"

"Very well," replied Duke with a nervous glance back at his unit mates.

"Carry on!" roared Tom.

Then, as Tom, Roger, and Astro sprawled on their bunks, grinning openly, the three Earthworm cadets began their simulated flight through space. Going through the movements of operating the complicated equipment of a spaceship, they pushed, pulled, jerked, snapped on imaginary switches, read unseen meters and gauges, and slammed around in their chairs to simulate acceleration reaction. The three cadets of the *Polaris* unit could no longer restrain themselves and broke into loud laughter at the antics of the aspirants. Finally, when they had landed their imaginary ship again, the Earthworms were pounded on the back heartily.

"Welcome to Space Academy!" said Tom with a grin. "That was as smooth a ride as I've ever had."

"Yeah," agreed Astro, pumping Coglin's hand. "You handled those reactors and atomic motors like a regular old space buster!"

"And that was real fine astrogation, Spears," Roger chimed in. "Why, you laid out such a smooth course, you never left the ground!"

The three Earthworms relaxed, and while Astro brewed hot cups of tea with synthetic pellets and water from the shower, Tom and Roger told them about the traditions and customs of the Academy.

Tom began by telling them how important it was for each crew member to be able to depend on his unit mate. "You see," he said, "in space there isn't much time for individual heroics. Too many things can happen too fast for it to be a one-man operation."

"I'll say," piped up Roger. "A couple of times I've been on the radar deck and seen a hunk of space junk coming down on us fast. So instead of following book procedure, relaying the dope to Tom on the control deck to pass it on to Astro, I'd just sing out to Astro direct on the intercom, 'Give me an upshot on the ecliptic!' or 'Give me a starboard shot!' and Astro would come through because he knows I always know what I'm talking about."

"Not always, hot-shot!" growled Astro. "How about the time we went out to Tara and snatched that hot copper

TOM CORBETT, SPACE CADET

asteroid out of Alpha Centauri's mouth? *You* said the time on that reactor blast should be set at—"[1]

"Is that so?" snapped Roger. "Listen, you big overgrown hunk of Venusian space gas—" Roger got no further. Astro grabbed him by the shirt front, held him at arm's length, and began tickling him in the ribs. The three freshmen cadets backed out of the way, glancing fearfully at the giant Venusian. Astro's strength was awesome when seen for the first time.

"Lemme go, you blasted space ape!" bellowed Roger, between fits of laughter.

"Say uncle, Manning!" roared Astro. "Promise you won't call me names again, or by the stars, I'll tickle you until you shake yourself apart!"

"All right—un-un-uncle!" managed Roger.

Astro dropped his unit mate on a bunk like a rag doll and turned back to Tom with a shrug of his shoulders. "He'll never learn, will he?"

Tom grinned at Duke. "Astro's like a big overgrown puppy."

"Someone ought to put him on a leash," growled Roger, crawling out of the bunk and rubbing his ribs. "Blast it, Astro, the next time you want to show off, go play with an elephant and leave me alone."

Astro ignored him, turning to Coglin. "As much as I gas Roger," the giant cadet said seriously, "I'd rather ride a thrust bucket with him on the radar deck than Commander Walters. He's the best."

Tom smiled. "That's what I mean, Duke. Astro believes in Roger, and Roger believes in Astro. I believe in them, and they in me. We've got to, or we wouldn't last long out there in space."

The three fledgling spacemen were silent, watching and listening with awe and envy as the *Polaris* crew continued their indoctrination. They considered themselves lucky to have been drawn by these famous cadets for their hazing.

---

[1] Astro is reminding Roger of a disastrous mistake that nearly spelled the end of the *Polaris* crew, recounted in the second book in the Tom Corbett, Space Cadet series: *Danger in Deep Space.*

The names of Corbett, Manning, and Astro were becoming synonymous with great adventure in space. But, with all their hairbreadth escapes, the *Polaris* unit was still just learning its job. The boys were still working off demerits, arguing with instructors on theory, listening to endless study spools, learning the latest advanced methods of astrogation, communication, and reactor-unit operation. They were working toward the day when they would discard the vivid blue uniforms of the Space Cadet Corps and don the magnificent black and gold of the Solar Guard.

Tom was aware of the eager expressions on the faces of the Earthworms and he smiled to himself. It was not a smile of smugness or conceit, but rather of honest satisfaction. More than once he had shaken his head in wonder at being a Space Cadet. The odds against it were enormous. Each year thousands of boys from all the major planets and the occupied satellites competed for entrance to the famed Academy and pitifully few were accepted. And he was happy at having two unit mates like Roger Manning and Astro to depend on when he was out in space, commanding one of the finest ships ever built, the powerful rocket cruiser *Polaris*.

As Roger and Astro continued to talk to the fledglings, Tom sipped his tea and thought of his own first days at the Academy. He remembered his fear and insecurity, and how hard he had fought to make what was then Unit 42-D a success, the unit that eventually became the *Polaris* unit. And how each assignment had brought him closer to his dream of becoming an officer in the Solar Guard.

He got up and walked to the window and looked out across the Academy campus, over the green lawns and white buildings connected by the rolling slidewalks, to the gleaming crystal Tower, the symbol of man's conquest of space. And beyond the Tower building, Tom saw a spaceship blasting off from the spaceport, her rockets bucking hard against thin air as she clawed her way spaceward. When it disappeared from sight, he followed it with his mind's eye and it became the *Polaris*, his ship! He and Roger and Astro were blasting through the cold black void, their own personal domain!

A loud burst of laughter behind him suddenly brought

Tom back to Earth. He smiled to himself and shook his head, as though reluctant to leave his dream world. He glanced out of the window again, this time down at the quadrangle, and far below he recognized the squat, muscular figure of Warrant Officer Mike McKenny drilling another group of newly arrived cadet candidates. Tom saw the slidewalks begin to fill with boys and men in varicolored uniforms, all released from duty as the day drew to a close. Tonight, Astro, Roger, and he would go to see the latest stereo, and tomorrow they would blast off in the *Polaris* for the weekly checkout of her equipment. He turned back to Spears, Coglin, and Duke. Roger was just finishing the story of their latest adventure.[2]

"The best part, of course, was the actual hunting of the tyrannosaurus," said Astro.

"A tyrannosaurus?" exploded Spears, the youngest and most impressionable of the three Earthworms. "You actually hunted for a dinosaur?"

Astro grinned. "That's right. They're extinct here on Earth, but on Venus we catch 'em and make pets out of the baby ones."

"We could have saved ourselves a lot of trouble, though," commented Roger mockingly. "We have several officers here that would have served just as well. Major 'Blast-off' Connel, for instance, the toughest, meanest old son of a hot rocket you have ever seen!"

"Stand to!"

The six boys nearly broke their backs jumping to attention. A squat, muscular figure, wearing the black-and-gold uniform of a Solar Guard, strode heavily into their line of vision. Roger gulped as Major Connel stopped in front of him. "Still gassing, eh, Manning?" he roared.

"'Evening, Major, sir," mumbled Roger, his face beet red. "We—er—ah—were just telling this Earthworm unit about the Academy, sir. Some of its pitfalls."

"Some of the cadets are going to fall into a pit if they don't learn to keep their mouths shut!" snapped Connel. He glared at Tom, Astro, and Roger, then wheeled sharply to

---

[2] Recounted in *The Revolt on Venus*, the fifth book in the series.

face the three quaking freshmen cadets. "You listen to any-thing they tell you and you'll wind up with a book full of demerits! What in blazes are you doing here, anyway? You're supposed to be at physical exams *right this minute!*"

The three boys began to shake visibly, not knowing whether to break ranks and run or wait until ordered.

"Get out of here!" Connel roared. "You've got thirty sec-onds to make it. And if you *don't* make it, you'll go down on my bad-rocket list!"

Almost in one motion, the three cadet candidates saluted and charged through the door. When they had gone, Connel turned to the *Polaris* cadets who were still at attention. "At ease!" he roared and then grinned.

The boys came to rest and smiled back at him tenta-tively. They never knew what to expect from Connel. "Well, did you put them through their paces?" he asked as he jerked his thumb toward the door.

"Yes, sir!" said Tom.

"Did they know their manual? Or give you any lip when you started giving them hot rockets?" Connel referred to the hazing that was allowed by the Academy, only as another of the multitude of tests given to cadets. Cadet candidates might possibly hide dangerous flaws from Academy officials but never from boys near their own ages.

"Major," said Astro, "those fellows came close to blasting off right here in these chairs. They really thought they were out in space!"

"Fine!" said Connel. "Glad to hear it. I've singled them out as my personal unit for instruction."

"Poor fellows," muttered Roger under his breath.

"What was that, Manning?" bellowed Connel.

"I said lucky fellows, sir," replied Roger innocently.

Connel glared at him. "I'll bet my last rocket that's what you said, Manning."

"Yes, sir."

Connel turned to the door and then spun around quickly to catch Roger grinning at Astro.

"'Poor fellows,' wasn't it?" said Connel with a grin.

Roger reddened and his unit mates laughed. "Oh, yes," continued Connel, "I almost forgot. Report to Commander

Walters on the double. You're getting special assignments. I recommended you for this job, so see that you behave yourselves. Especially you, Manning."

He turned and disappeared through the doorway, leaving the three cadets staring at each other.

"Wowie!" yelled Astro. "And I thought we were going to get chewed up for keeping those Earthworms too long!"

"Same here," said Roger.

"Wonder what the assignment is?" said Tom, grabbing his tunic and racing for the door. Neither Roger nor Astro answered as they followed on his heels. When they reached the slidestairs, a moving belt of plastic that spiraled upward to an overhead slidewalk bridge connecting the dormitory to the Tower of Galileo, Tom's eyes were bright and shiny. "Whatever it is," he said, "if Major Connel suggested us for it, you can bet your last reactor it'll be a rocket-buster."

As the boys stepped on the slidestairs that would take them to Commander Walters' office, each of them was very much aware that this was the first step to a new adventure in space. And though the three realized that they could expect danger, the special assignment meant that they were going to hit the high, wide, and deep again. And that was all they asked of life. To be in space, a spaceman's only real home!

2 "GENTLEMEN, PLEASE!"

COMMANDER WALTERS, THE COMMANDANT OF SPACE Academy, stood behind his desk and slammed his fist down sharply on its plastic top. "I must insist that you control your tempers and refrain from these repeated outbursts," he growled.

The angry voices that had filled the room began to subside, but Walters did not continue his address. He stood, arms folded across his chest, glaring at the assembled group of men until, one by one, they stopped talking and shifted nervously in their chairs. When the room was finally still, the commander glanced significantly at Captain Steve Strong, standing at the side of the desk, smiled grimly, and then resumed in a calm, conversational tone of voice.

"I am quite aware that we have departed from standard operational procedure in this case," he said slowly. "Heretofore, the Solar Guard has always granted interplanetary shipping contracts to private companies on the basis of sealed bids, the most reasonable bid winning the job. However, for the job of hauling Titan crystal to Earth, we have found that method unsatisfactory. Therefore, we have devised this new plan to select the right company. And let me repeat"—Walters leaned forward over his desk and spoke in a firm, decisive voice—"this decision was reached in a special executive session of the Council of the Solar Alliance last night."

A short, wiry man suddenly rose from his chair in the front row, his face clearly showing his displeasure. "All right, get on with it, Walters!" he snapped, deliberately omitting the courtesy of addressing the commander by his title. "Don't waste our time with that 'official' hogwash. It might work on your cadets and your tin soldiers, but not on us!"

There was a murmur of agreement from the assembled group of men. Present were some of the wealthiest and most powerful shipping magnates in the entire Solar Alliance— men who controlled vast fleets of commercial spaceships and whose actions and decisions carried a great deal of weight. Each hoped to win the Solar Guard contract to transport Titan crystal from the mines on the tiny satellite[3] back to Earth. Combining steel-like strength and durability with its great natural beauty, the crystal was replacing metal in all construction work and the demand was enormous. The shipping company that got the job would have a guaranteed income for years to come, and each of the men

---

[3] Titan, the largest of Saturn's 62 satellites, is the second largest moon in our solar system (after Jupiter's Ganymede), and the only moon known to have a dense atmosphere. Titan is also the only celestial object besides earth with clear evidence of stable bodies of surface liquid.

present was fighting with every weapon at his command to win the contract.

Heartened by the reaction of the men around him, the speaker pressed his advantage. "We've all hauled cargo for the Solar Guard before, and the sealed-bid system was perfectly satisfactory then!" he shouted. "Why isn't it satisfactory now? What's all this nonsense about a space race?"

Again, the murmur filled the room and the men glared accusingly at Walters. But the commander refused to knuckle down to any show of arrogance. He fixed a cold, stony eye on the short man. "Mr. Brett," he snapped in a biting voice, "you have been invited to this meeting as a guest, not by any right you think you have as the owner of a shipping company. A guest, I said, and I ask that you conduct yourself with that social obligation in mind!"

Before Brett could reply, Walters turned away from him and addressed the others calmly. "Despite Mr. Brett's outburst, his question is a good one. And the answer is quite simple. The bids submitted by your companies were not satisfactory in this case because we believe that they were made in bad faith!"

For once, there was silence in the room as the men stared at Walters in shocked disbelief. "There are fourteen shipping companies represented in this room, some of them the most respected in the Solar Alliance," he continued, his voice edged with knifelike sarcasm. "I cannot find it in my conscience to accuse all of you of complicity in this affair, but nevertheless we are faced with one of the most startling coincidences I have ever seen."

Walters paused and looked around the room, measuring the effect of his words. Satisfied, he went on grimly, "There isn't enough difference between the bids of each of you, not *five credits'* worth of difference, to award the contract to any single company!"

The men in the room gasped in amazement.

"The bids were exactly alike. The only differences we found were in operational procedure. But the cost to the Solar Guard amounted to, in the end, exactly the same thing from each of you! The inference is clear, I believe," he added mockingly. "Someone stole the minimum specifications and circulated them among you."

In the shocked quiet that followed Walters' statement, no one noticed Tom, Roger, and Astro slip into the room. They finally caught the eye of Captain Strong, who acknowledged their presence with a slight nod, as they found seats in the rear of the room.

"Commander," a voice spoke up from the middle of the group, "may I make a statement?"

"Certainly, Mr. Barnard," agreed Walters, and stepped back from his desk as a tall, slender man in his late thirties rose to address the men around him. The three Space Cadets stared at him with interest. They had heard of Kit Barnard. A former Solar Guard officer, he had resigned from the great military organization to go into private space-freight business. Though a newcomer, with only a small outfit, he was well liked and respected by every man in the room. And everyone present knew that when he spoke, he would have something important to say, or at least advance a point that should be brought to light.

"I have no doubt," said Barnard in a slow, positive manner, "that the decision to substitute a space race between us as a means of awarding the contract was well considered by the Solar Council." He turned and shot Brett a flinty look. "And under the circumstances, I, for one, accept their decision." He sat down abruptly.

There were cries of: "Hear! Hear!" "Righto!" "Very good!"

"No!" shouted Brett, leaping to his feet. "By the craters of Luna, it isn't right! I demand to know exactly who submitted the lowest bid!"

Walters sighed and shuffled through several papers on his desk. "You are within your rights, Mr. Brett," he said, eying the man speculatively. "It was you."

"Then why in blue blazes didn't I get the contract?" screamed Brett.

"For several reasons," replied Walters. "Your contract offered us the lowest bid in terms of money, but specified very slow schedules. On the other hand, Universal Spaceways Limited planned faster schedules, but at a higher cost. Kit Barnard outbid both of you in money and schedules, but he has only two ships, and we were doubtful of his ability to complete the contract should one of his ships crack up. The other companies offered, more or less, the same conditions. So you can understand our decision now, Mr. Brett." Walters paused and glared at the man. "The Solar Council sat in a continuous forty-eight-hour session and considered *everyone*. The space race was finally decided on, and voted for by every member. Schedules were the most vital point under consideration. But other points could not be ignored, and these could only be determined by actual performance. Now, does that answer all your questions, Mr. Brett?"

"No, it doesn't!" yelled Brett.

"Oh, sit down, Brett!" shouted a voice from the back of the room.

"Yes! Sit down and shut up!" called another. "We're in this too, you know!"

Brett turned on them angrily, but finally sat down, scowling.

In the rear of the room Tom nudged Roger. "Boy! The commander sure knows how to lay it on the line when he wants to, doesn't he?"

"I'll say!" replied Roger. "That guy Brett better watch out. Both the commander and Captain Strong look as if they're ready to pitch him out on his ear."

Six feet tall, and looking crisp, sure, and confident in his black-and-gold uniform, Captain Steve Strong stood near Walters and scowled at Brett. Unit instructor for the *Polaris* crew and Commander Walters' executive officer, Strong was not as adept as Walters in masking his feelings, and his face clearly showed his annoyance at Brett's outbursts. He had sat the full forty-eight hours with the Council while they argued, not over costs, but in an effort to make sure that none of the companies would be slighted in their final decision. It made his blood boil to see someone like Brett selfishly disregard these efforts at fairness.

"That is all the information I can give you, gentlemen," said Walters finally. "Thank you for your kind attention"—he shot an ironic glance at Brett— "and for your understanding of a difficult situation. Now you must excuse me. Captain Strong, whom you all know, will fill in the details of the race."

As Walters left the room, Strong stepped to the desk, faced the assembly, and spoke quickly. "Gentlemen, perhaps some of you are acquainted with the present jet car race that takes place each year? The forerunner of that race was the Indianapolis Five-Hundred-Mile Race of some few hundred years ago. We have adopted their rules for our own speed tests. Time trials will be held with all interested companies contributing as many ships that they think can qualify, and the three ships that make the fastest time will be entered in the actual race. This way we can eliminate the weaker contenders and reduce the chance of accidents taking place millions of miles out in space. Also, it will result in a faster time for the winner. Now, the details of the race will be given to your chief pilots, crew chiefs, and power-deck officers at a special meeting in my office here in the Tower building tomorrow. You will receive all information and regulations governing the minimum and maximum size of the ships entered, types of reactor units, and amount of ballast to be carried."

"How many in the crew?" asked a man in the front.

"Two," replied Steve, "or if the ship is mostly automatic, one. Either can be used. The Solar Guard will monitor the race, sending along one of the heavy cruisers." Strong glanced at his notes. "That is all, gentlemen. Are there any questions?"

There were no questions and the men began to file out of the room. Strong was relieved to see Brett was among the first to leave. He didn't trust himself to keep his temper with the man. As the room emptied, Strong stood at the door and grabbed Kit Barnard by the sleeve. "Hello, spaceman!" he cried. "Long time, no see!"

"Hello, Steve," replied Kit, with a slow, warm smile.

"Say! Is that the way to greet an old friend after four, or is it five years?"

"Five," replied Kit.

"You look worried, fellow," said Strong.

"I am. This race business leaves me holding the bag."

"How's that?"

"Well, I made a bid on the strength of a new reactor unit I'm trying to develop," explained Kit. "If I had gotten the contract, I could have made a loan from the Universal Bank and completed my work easily. But now—" Kit stopped and shook his head slowly.

"What is this reactor?" Strong asked. "Something new?"

"Yes. One quarter the size of present standard reactors and less than half the weight." Kit's eyes began to glow with enthusiasm as he spoke. "It would give me extra space in my ships and be economical enough on fuel for me to be able to compete with the larger outfits and their bigger ships. Now, all I've got is a reactor that hasn't been tested properly, that I'm not even sure will work on a long haul and a hot race."

"Is there any way you can soup up one of your present reactors to make this run?" asked Strong.

"I suppose so," added Kit. "I'll give the other fellows a run for their money all right. But it'll take every credit I have. And if I don't win the race, I'm finished. Washed up."

"Excuse me, Captain Strong," said Tom Corbett, coming to attention. "Major Connel ordered us to report here for special assignment."

"Oh, yes," said Strong, turning to Tom, Roger, and Astro with a smile. "Meet Kit Barnard. Kit—Tom Corbett, Roger Manning, and Astro, the *Polaris* unit. My unit," he added proudly.

The boys saluted respectfully, and Barnard smiled and shook hands with each of them.

"You've heard about the race now," said Strong to Tom.

"Yes, sir," replied the young cadet. "It sounds exciting."

"It will be, with spacemen like Kit Barnard, Charley Brett, and the other men of the big outfits competing. You're going to work with me on the time trials, and later the *Polaris* will be the ship that monitors the race. But first, you three will be inspectors."

"Of what, sir?" asked Roger.

"You'll see that all regulations are observed—that no one gets the jump on anyone else. These men will be souping up their reactors until those ships will be nothing but 'go,' and it's your job to see that they use only standard equipment."

"We're going to be real popular when we tell a spaceman he can't use a unit he's rigged up specially," commented Astro with a grin.

Tom laughed. "We'll be known as the cadets you love to hate!"

"Especially when you run up against Charley Brett," said Kit.

The cadets looked at the veteran spaceman inquiringly, but he was not smiling, and they suddenly felt a strange chill of apprehension.

3 "IT'S ABOUT TIME YOU GOT HERE!" CHARLEY BRETT GLARED ANGRILY AT HIS CHIEF PILOT,

Quent Miles, as he sauntered into the office and flopped into a chair.

"I had a heavy date last night. I overslept," the spaceman replied, yawning loudly.

"We're late for Strong's meeting over at the Academy," Brett snapped. "Get up! We've got to leave right away."

Quent Miles looked at the other man, his black eyes gleaming coldly. "I'll get up when I'm ready," he said slowly.

The two men glared at each other for a moment, and finally Brett lowered his eyes. Miles grinned and yawned again.

"Come on," said Brett in a less demanding tone. "Let's go. No use getting Strong down on us before we even get started."

"Steve Strong doesn't scare me," replied Miles.

"All right! He doesn't scare you. He doesn't scare me, either," said Brett irritably. "Now that we both know that neither of us is scared, let's get going."

Quent smiled again and rose slowly. "You know

something, Charley?" he said in a deceptively mild voice. "One of these days you're going to get officious with the wrong spaceman, one that isn't as tolerant as I am, and you're going to be pounded into space dust."

Quent Miles stood in front of Brett's desk and stretched like a languid cat. Brett noted the powerful hands and arms and the depth of the shoulders and chest, all emphasized by the tight-fitting clothes the spaceman affected. The man was dark and swarthy, and dressed all in black. Brett had often imagined that if the devil ever took human form it would look like Quent Miles. He shivered uncontrollably and waited. Finally Miles turned to him, a mocking smile on his face.

"Well, Charley? What are we waiting for?"

A few moments later they were speeding through the broad streets of Atom City in a jet cab on the way to the Atom City spaceport.

"What's this all about?" demanded Quent, settling back in his seat. "Why the rush call?"

"I didn't get the contract to haul the crystal," replied Brett grimly. "All the bids were so close the Solar Council decided to have a space race out to Titan to pick the outfit that would get the job."

Quent turned toward him, surprised. "But I thought you had all that sewed up tight!" he exclaimed. "I thought after you got your hands on the—"

"Shut up!" interrupted Brett. "The details on the specifications leaked out. Now the only way I can get the contract is to win the race."

"And I'm the guy to do it?" asked Quent with a smile.

"That's what you're here for. If we don't win this race, we're finished. Washed up!"

"Who else is in the race?"

"Every other major space-freight outfit in the system," replied Brett grimly. "And Kit Barnard."

"Has Barnard got that new reactor of his working yet?"

"I don't think so. But I have no way of telling."

"If he has, you're not going to win this race," said Quent, shaking his head. "Nor is anyone else."

"You are here for one reason," said Brett pointedly.

"I know." Quent grinned. "To win a race."

"Right."

Quent laughed. "With those heaps you've fooled people into thinking are spaceships? Don't make me laugh."

"There are going to be time trials before the race," said Brett. "The three fastest ships are going to make the final run. I'm not worried about the race itself. I've got a plan that will assure us of winning. It's the time trials that's got me bothered."

"Leave that to me," said Quent.

The jet cab pulled up to the main gate of the spaceport and the two men got out. Far across the field, a slender, needle-nosed ship stood poised on her stabilizer fins ready for flight. She was black except for a red band painted on the hull across the forward section and around the few viewports. It gave her the appearance of a huge laughing insect. Quent eyed the vessel with a practiced eye.

"I'll have to soup her up," he commented. "She wouldn't win a foot race now."

"Don't depend too heavily on your speed," said Brett. "I would just as soon win by default. After all," he continued, looking at Miles with calculating eyes, "serious accidents could delay the other ships."

"Sure. I know what you mean," replied the spaceman.

"Good!" Brett turned away abruptly and headed for the ship. Quent following him. In a little while the white-hot exhaust flare from the rocket tubes of the sleek ship splattered the concrete launching apron and it lifted free of the ground. Like an evil, predatory bug, the ship blasted toward the Academy spaceport.

"WELL, BLAST MY JETS!" Astro gasped, stopping in his tracks and pointing. Tom and Roger looked out over the quadrangle toward the Academy spaceport where ship after ship, braking jets blasting, sought the safety of the ground.

"Great galaxy," exclaimed Tom, his eyes bulging, "there must be a hundred ships!"

"At least," commented Roger.

"But they can't all be here for the trials," said Astro.

"Why not?" asked Roger. "This is a very important race.

Who knows what ship might win? It pays the company to enter every ship they have."

"Roger's right, Astro," said Tom. "These fellows are playing for big stakes. Though I don't think there'll be more than thirty or forty ships in the actual speed trials. See those big-bellied jobs? They're repair ships."

"I hadn't thought about that," acknowledged the big Venusian cadet. "They'll probably be jazzing up those sleek babies and that takes a lot of repair and work."

"Come on," said Tom. "We've got to get over to the meeting. Captain Strong said he wanted us to be there."

The three cadets turned back toward the nearest slide-walk and hopped on. None of them noticed the black ship with the red band around its bow which suddenly appeared over the field, rockets blasting loudly as it began to drop expertly to the ground.

From early morning the skies over the Academy had been vibrating to the thunderous exhausts of the incoming fleet of ships. Painted with company colors and insignia, the ships landed in allotted space on the field, and almost immediately, mechanics, crew chiefs, and specialists of all kinds swarmed over the space vessels preparing them for the severest tests they would ever undergo. The ships that actually were to make the trial runs were stripped of every spare pound of weight, while their reactors were taken apart and specially designed compression heads were put on the atomic motors.

The entire corps of Space Cadets had been given a special three-day holiday to see the trials, and the Academy buildings were decorated with multicolored flags and pennants. A festive atmosphere surrounded the vast Solar Guard installation.

But in his office in the Tower of Galileo, Captain Strong paced the floor, a worried frown on his face. He stepped around his desk and picked up a paper to re-read it for the tenth time. He shook his head and flipped open the key of his desk intercom, connecting him with the enlisted spaceman in the next office.

"Find Kit Barnard, spaceman!" Strong called. "And give him an oral message. *Personal.* Tell him I said he can't use his reactor unit unless he changes it to more standard operational design." Strong paused and glanced at the paper again. "As it stands now, his reactor will not be approved for the trials," he continued. "Tell him he has until midnight tonight to submit new specifications."

As Strong closed the intercom key abruptly, the three members of the *Polaris* unit stepped into his office and saluted smartly. Strong looked up. "Hello, boys. Sit down." He waved them to nearby chairs and turned back to his desk. The drawn expression of their unit commander did not go unnoticed.

"Is there something wrong, sir?" asked Tom tentatively.

"Nothing much," replied Strong wearily. He indicated the sheaf of papers in front of him. "These are reactor-unit specifications submitted by the pilots and crew chiefs of the ships to be flown in the time trials. I've just had to reject Kit Barnard's specifications."

"What was the matter?" asked Astro.

"Not enough safety allowance. He's running too close to the danger point in feeding reactant to the chambers, using D-18 rate of feed and D-9 is standard."

"What about the other ships, sir?" asked Tom. "Do they all have safety factors?"

Strong shrugged his shoulders. "They all specify standard reaction rates without actually using figures," he said. "But I'm certain that their feeders are being tuned up for maximum output. That's where your job is going to come in. You've got to inspect the ships to make sure they're safe."

"Then Kit Barnard put down his specifications, knowing that there was a chance they wouldn't pass," Tom remarked.

Strong nodded. "He's an honest man."

The door opened and several men stepped inside. They were dressed in the mode of merchant space officers, wearing high-peaked hats, trim jackets, and trousers of a different color. Strong stood up to greet them.

"Welcome, gentlemen. Please be seated. We will begin the meeting as soon as all the pilots are here."

Roger nudged Astro and whispered, "What's the big deal about a D-18 rate and a D-9 rate? Why is that so important?"

"It has to do with the pumps," replied the power-deck cadet. "They cool the reactant fuel to keep it from getting too hot and wildcatting. At a D-9 rate the reactant is hot enough to create power for normal flight. Feeding at a D-18 rate is fine too, but you need pumps to cool the motors, and pumps that could do the job would be too big."

"Kit's problem," commented Tom, "is not so much building the reactor, but a cooling system to keep it under control."

"Will that make a big difference in who wins the race?" asked Roger.

"With that ship of Kit's," said Astro, shaking his head, "I doubt if he'll be able to come even close to the top speeds in the trials unless he can use the new reactor."

The room had filled up now and Strong rapped on the desk for attention.

He stared at the faces of the men before him, men who had spent their lives in space. They were the finest pilots and crew chiefs in the solar system. They sat quietly and attentively as Strong gave them the details of the greatest race of spaceships in over a hundred years.

After Strong had outlined the plans for the time trials, he concluded, "Each of you competing in the time trials will be given a blast-off time and an orbital course. Only standard, Solar-Guard-approval equipment will be allowed in the tests. I will monitor the trials, and Space Cadets Corbett, Manning, and Astro will be in complete charge of all inspections of your ships." Strong paused and looked around. "Are there any questions?"

"When will the first ship blast off, Captain Strong?" asked a lean and leathery-looking spaceman in the back of the room.

"First time trial takes place at 0600 hours tomorrow morning. Each ship has a designated time. Consult your schedules for the blast-off time of your ships."

"What if a ship isn't ready?" asked Kit Barnard, who had slipped into the room unnoticed.

"Any ship unable to blast off at scheduled time," said Strong, finding it difficult to look at his old friend, "will be eliminated."

There was a sudden murmur in the room and Quent Miles rose quickly. "That's not much time to prepare our ships," he said. "I don't know who's going to be first, but I can't even strip my ship by tomorrow morning, let alone soup up the reactant." His voice was full of contempt, and he glanced around the room at the other pilots. "Seems to me we're being treated a little roughly."

There were several cries of agreement.

Strong held up his hand. "Gentlemen, I know it is difficult to prepare a ship in twelve hours for a race as important as this one," he said. "But I personally believe that any spaceman who really wants to make it *can* make it!"

"Well, I'm not going to break my back to make a deadline," snarled Quent. "And I don't think any of the other fellows here will either."

"If you are scheduled to blast off tomorrow at 0600 hours, Captain Miles," Strong announced coldly, "and you are unable to raise ship, you will be eliminated."

Stifling an angry retort, Quent Miles sat down, and while Strong continued to answer questions, Astro, a worried frown on his face, stared at the spaceman dressed in black. Tom noticed it. "What's wrong with you, Astro?" he asked.

"That spaceman Miles," replied Astro. "I could swear I know him, yet I'm sure that I don't."

"He's not a very ordinary-looking guy," observed Roger. "He's plenty big and he's so dark that it wouldn't be easy to mistake him."

"Still," said Astro, screwing up his forehead, "I know I've seen him before."

"If there are no further questions, gentlemen," said Strong, "we'll close this meeting. I know you're anxious to get to your ships and begin work. But before you go, I would like to introduce the cadet inspectors to you. Stand up, boys."

Self-consciously, Tom, Roger, and Astro stood up while Strong addressed the pilots.

"Cadet Manning will be in charge of all electronics inspections, Cadet Astro in charge of the power deck, and Cadet Corbett will cover the control deck and overall inspection of the ship itself."

Quent Miles was on his feet again, shouting, "Do you mean to tell me that we're going to be told what we can and can't do by those three kids!" He turned and glared at Tom. "You come messing around my ship, buster, and you'll be pitched out on your ear!"

"If the cadets do not pass on your ship," said Strong, with more than a little edge to his voice, "it will not get off the ground."

The two men locked eyes across the room.

"We'll see about that!" growled Miles, and stalked from the room, his heavy shoulders swinging from side to side in an exaggerated swagger.

"I believe that's all, gentlemen," announced Strong coldly, "and spaceman's luck to each of you."

After the men had left, the three cadets crowded around Strong. "Do you think we'll have any trouble with Miles, sir?" asked Tom.

"You have your orders, Tom," said Strong. "If any ship does not meet standards established for the race, it will be disqualified!"

Astro stared at the doorway through which Quent Miles had disappeared. He scratched his head and muttered, "If it wasn't for just one thing, I'd swear by the stars that he's the same spaceman who—" He stopped and shook his head.

"Who what?" asked Strong.

"Nothing, sir," said Astro. "I *must* be mistaken. It can't be the same man."

"I suggest that you sleep out at the spaceport tonight," said Strong. "The first ship will have to be inspected before she blasts off, and that means you will have to look her over before six."

"Yes, sir," replied Tom.

"And watch out for Quent Miles," warned Strong.

"Yes, sir," said the curly-haired cadet. "I know what you mean."

4 "THE COURSE IS TO LUNA AND RETURN! SPACE-MAN'S LUCK." Captain Strong's voice rasped out over the public-address system as a lone spaceship stood poised on the starting ramp, her ports closed, her crew making last-minute preparations. Ringing the huge space-port, crews from other ships paused in their work to watch the first vessel make the dash around the Moon in a frantic race against the astral chronometer. In the temporary grandstands at the north end of the field, thousands of spectators from cities all over Earth leaned forward, hushed and expectant.

"Are you ready *Star Lady?*" Strong called, his voice echoing over the field.

A light flashed from the viewport of the ship.

"Stand by to raise ship!" roared Strong. "Blast off, minus five, four, three, two, one— *zero!*"

There was a sudden, ear-shattering roar and smoke and flame poured from the exhaust of the ship, spilling over the blast-off ramp. The ship rocked from side to side gently, rose into the air slowly, and then gathering speed began to move spaceward. In a moment it was gone and only the echoing blasts of thunder from its exhausts remained.

"There goes number one," said Tom to his unit mates as they watched from a vantage point near one of the service hangars.

"He got a pretty shaky start there at the ramp," commented Astro. "He must've poured on so much power, he couldn't control the ship."

"Heads up, fellas," announced Roger suddenly. "Here comes work." Kit Barnard was walking toward them, carrying a small metallic object in his hand.

"Morning, boys," said Kit with a weary smile. His eyes were bloodshot.

The cadets knew he had worked all night to revise and resubmit his specification sheet to Strong.

"'Morning, sir," said Tom.

"I'd like to have you OK this gear unit. I made it last night."

Astro took the gear and examined it closely.

"Looks fine to me," he said finally, handing it back. "Part of your main pumps?"

"Why, yes," replied Kit, surprised. "Say, you seem to know your business."

"Only the best rocket-buster in space, sir," chimed in Tom. "He eats, sleeps, and dreams about machinery on a power deck."

"Is that for your new reactor, sir?" asked Astro.

"Yes. Want to come over and take a look at it?"

"Want to!" exclaimed Roger. "You couldn't keep him away with a ray gun, Captain Barnard."

"Fine," said Kit. "Incidentally, I'm not in the Solar Guard any more; don't even hold a reserve commission, so you don't have to 'sir' me. I'd prefer just plain Kit. OK?"

The three boys grinned. "OK, Kit," said Tom.

Astro began to fidget and Tom nudged Roger. "Think we can spare the Venusian for a little while?"

"Might as well let him go," grunted Roger. "He'd only sneak off later, anyway."

Astro grinned sheepishly. "If anyone wants me to check anything, I'll be over at Kit's. Where is your ship?" he asked the veteran spaceman.

"Hangar Fourteen. Opposite the main entrance gate."

"Fine, that's where I'll be, fellows. See you later."

With Astro bending over slightly to hear what Kit was

saying, the two men walked away. Roger shook his head. "You know, I still can't get used to that guy. He acts like a piece of machinery was a good-looking space doll!"

"I've seen you look the same way at your radarscope, Roger."

"Yeah, but it's different with me."

"Is it?" said Tom, turning away so that Roger would not see him laughing. And as he did, he saw something that made him pause. In front of the hangar, Captain Strong was talking to Quent Miles. There was no mistaking the tall spaceman in his severe black clothes.

"Here comes more work," muttered Tom. Quent had turned away from Strong and was walking toward them.

"Strong said I had to get you to OK this scope," said Quent with a sneer. "Hurry it up! I haven't got all day."

He handed them a radarscope that was common equipment on small pleasure yachts, and was considerably lighter in weight than the type used on larger freight vessels.

"What's the gross weight of your ship?" asked Roger after a quick glance at the large glass tube with a crystal surface that had been polished to a smooth finish.

"Two thousand tons," said Quent. "Why?"

Roger shook his head. "This is too small, Mr. Miles. You will have to use the standard operational scope."

"But it's too big."

"I'm sorry, sir—" began Roger.

"Sorry!" Quent exploded. "Give me that tube, you squirt." He snatched it out of Roger's hand. "I'm using this scope whether you like it or not!"

"If you use that scope," said Tom coldly, "your ship will be disqualified."

Quent glared at the two boys for a moment, his black

eyes cold and hard. "They make kids feel mighty important around here, don't they?"

"They give us jobs to do," said Roger. "Usually we can handle them fine. Occasionally we run into a space-gassing bum and he makes things difficult, but we manage to take care of him."

Quent stepped forward in a threatening manner, but Roger did not move. "Listen," the spaceman snarled, "stay out of my way, you young punk, or I'll blast you."

"Don't ever make the mistake of touching me, Mister," said Roger calmly. "You might find that you're the one who's blasted."

Quent stared at them a moment, then spun on his heels and swaggered back to his ship.

"You know, Roger," said Tom, watching Miles disappear into the hangar, "I have an idea he is one spaceman who'll back up his threats."

Roger ignored Tom's statement. "Come on. We've got a lot of work to do," he said, turning away.

The two cadets headed for the next hangar and boarded a ship with the picture of a chicken on its nose. While Roger examined the communications and astrogation deck, Tom busied himself inspecting the control deck, where the great panels of the master control board were stripped of everything but absolute essentials. Later, they called Astro back to make a careful inspection of the power deck on the ship. While they waited for the Venusian cadet, Tom and Roger talked to the pilot.

Gigi Duarte was a small, dapper Frenchman who somehow, in the course of his life, had acquired the nickname "Chicken" and it had been with him ever since. The cadets had met him once before when they rode on a passenger liner from Mars to Venusport and liked the small, stubby spaceman. Now, renewing their friendship, the boys and "Gigi the Chicken" sat on the lower step of the airlock and chatted.

"This is the greatest thing that has happened to me," said Gigi. "Ever since I can remember, I have wanted to race in space!"

"Don't get much chance when you're hauling passengers

around, I guess," said Tom.

Gigi shook his head. "One must always be careful. Just so fast, over a certain route, taking all the precautionary steps for fuel! Bah! But this flight! This time, I will show you speed! Watch the French Chicken and you will see speed as you have never—" Suddenly he stopped and frowned. "But you cannot see me. I will be going too fast!"

Tom and Roger laughed. After Astro joined them, they shook hands with the Frenchman, wished him luck, and went to the next ship to inspect it. Gigi's ship was already being towed out to the blast-off ramp, and by the time the three boys had completed their inspection of the next ship, the gaily colored French ship flashed the ready signal to Strong.

"Blast off, minus five, four, three, two, one—*zero!*" Strong's voice boomed out over the loudspeakers and the French Chicken poured on the power. His ship arose from the ground easily, and in five seconds was out of sight in the cloudless skies above.

ALL DAY THE SPACEPORT ROCKED with the thunderous noise of stripped-down spaceships blasting off on their trial runs around the Moon. Kit Barnard worked like a demon to complete the cooling system in his aged ship, and as each ship blasted off on its scheduled run to the Moon, the time for his own flight drew nearer. Kit worked with his chief crewman, Sid Goldberg, a serious, swarthy-faced youngster who rivaled Astro in his love for the power-deck machinery on a spaceship. By nightfall, with Tom, Roger, and Astro standing by to make their final inspection, Kit wiped the oil and grime from his hands and stepped back. "Well, she's finished.

You can make your inspections now, boys," he said.

While Tom, Astro, and Roger swarmed over the vessel, examining the newly designed and odd-looking gear, the veteran spaceman and his young helper stretched out on the concrete ramp and in thirty seconds were asleep.

The *Polaris* unit quickly checked out Kit's ship as qualified for the race, and then turned, fascinated, to the tangle of pipes, cables, and mechanical gear of the reactor unit and cooling pumps. Tom and Roger were unable to figure out exactly what changes Kit had made, but Astro gazed at the new machinery fondly, almost rapturously. He tried to explain the intricate work to his unit mates, but would stop in the middle of a sentence when a new detail of the construction would catch his eye.

"Come on, Roger," Tom sighed. "Let's go on to the next ship. This lovesick Venusian can catch up with us later."

They turned away and left Astro alone on the power deck, doubtful that he had even noticed their departure.

The trials had been suspended at nightfall, and the ships that had already blasted off left sections of the huge spaceport empty. The day had been a grueling one for the cadets, and Tom and Roger climbed wearily on the nearest slidewalk that would take them back to the Academy grounds. Just as they rode through the main field gate, Roger nudged Tom. "Look! There's Quent Miles up ahead of us," he said. "Isn't he scheduled to blast off in the morning?"

"Yes. Why?" asked Tom.

"He hasn't called us in to inspect his ship yet."

"Maybe he isn't ready yet," said Tom. "Probably still souping it up."

"I've been watching him. He hasn't done very much."

"What do you mean?"

"He's the only one working on his ship," replied Roger. "Not one helper."

Tom snorted. "You're beginning to suspect everything, Roger. He might be going to get a part or grab a bite to eat."

"Where? In Atom City?" asked Roger. "That's the slidewalk to the monorail station." He pointed to the black-suited figure as he hopped on another moving belt that angled away from theirs.

"Oh, forget it," groaned Tom. "I'm too tired to think about it now. Let's just report to Captain Strong and get some sack time. I'm all out of reactant."

"I suppose Astro will spend half the night trying to figure out what it took Kit Barnard years to build," mused Roger.

"And if I know Astro," chuckled Tom, "he'll get it figured out too!"

As the two weary cadets continued their ride into the

Academy grounds, on another slidewalk going in the opposite direction, Quent Miles watched the darkening countryside closely. It was several miles from the Academy to the monorail station, and the moving belt dipped and turned through the rugged country that surrounded Space Academy. Suddenly Quent straightened, and making certain no one was watching him, he jumped off the slidewalk and hurried to a clump of bushes a few hundred yards away. He disappeared into the thick foliage and then reached inside his tunic and pulled out a paralo-ray gun.

"You in here, Charley?" Miles whispered.

There was a movement to his left and he leveled the gun. "All right! Come out of there!"

The bushes parted and Charley Brett stepped out. "Put that thing away!" he snarled. "What's that for?"

"After I got your message to meet you out here, I didn't know what was up, so I brought this along just in case," Quent replied. "What's so secret that you couldn't come to the spaceport?"

"I've got the stuff for Kit Barnard's reactor."

"What stuff?"

"This." Brett took a small lead container out of his pocket and handed it to Quent. "This is impure reactant. Dump it into his feeders and we can count him out of the race."

Quent took the lead container, looked at it, and then stuffed it inside his tunic. "What'll happen?"

"Nothing. He'll just get out in space and find his pumps won't handle the heat from his feeders, that's all. He's the only one I'm worried about."

"Reports are coming in from Luna City. You can worry about Gigi Duarte, too. He's burning up space."

"Ross is at the Luna spaceport," replied Brett. "He'll take care of any ship that looks like it's going to be too fast."

"Then why not have him take care of Kit Barnard too?" demanded Quent. "There will be less chance of getting caught. Remember, I've got those three Space Cadets and Strong to worry about."

"You can't expect to get what we're after unless you take chances. Now get back to the spaceport and put this stuff in Barnard's feeders. You blast off tomorrow morning before he does and won't have much time."

"OK," agreed Quent. "When did Ross get to Luna City?"

"Yesterday. I had him come in from the hide-out."

"You think there'll be any cause for suspicion with him on the Moon and me down here?" asked Quent.

"When you land at Luna City spaceport, he'll disappear. By that time we should know how the time trials are shaping up."

"OK Where are you going now?"

"Back to the office. I've still got some things to check on before the big race. We're going to use the hideout for that."

A smile spread across Quent Miles' face. "So that's it, eh? Pretty clever, Charley. Ross know about it?"

"Yeah. He's leaving as soon as he knows we've won the time trials. Now get back to the spaceport and take care of Barnard's ship."

Quent slipped his hand inside his tunic and patted the lead container. "Too bad this isn't a baby bomb," he muttered. "We could be sure Barnard wouldn't finish."

"He's finished right now, but he doesn't know it." Brett smiled. "He's borrowed heavily just on this race, and when he loses, the banks will close him up. Kit Barnard is through."

5 "WE REGRET TO ANNOUNCE THAT THE SPACESHIP *LA BELLE FRANCE*, PILOTED BY GIGI DUARTE, HAS CRASHED."** Captain Strong's voice was choked with emotion as he made the announcement over the spaceport public-address system. There was an audible groan of sympathy from the thousands of spectators in the grandstands. In spite of every precaution for safety, death had visited the spaceways.

Strong continued, "We have just received official confirmation from Luna City that the Paris-Venusport Transfer Company entry exploded in space soon after leaving Luna City. Captain Duarte had flown the first leg of the race from Earth to the Moon in record time."

The Solar Guard officer snapped off the microphone and turned to Tom, Roger, and Astro. "It's hard to believe that the French Chicken won't be shuttling from Paris to Venusport any more," he murmured.

"Are there any details, sir?" asked Tom.

"You know there are never any details, Corbett," said Strong with a little edge in his voice. Then he immediately apologized. "I'm sorry, Tom. Gigi was an old friend."

The door behind them opened and an enlisted spaceman stepped inside, saluting smartly. "Ready for the next blast-off, Captain Strong," he announced.

"Who is it?" asked Strong, turning to the intercom connecting him with the control tower that coordinated all the landings and departures at the spaceport.

The spaceman referred to a clipboard. "It's the *Space Lance*, sir. Piloted by Captain Sticoon. He's representing an independent company from Marsopolis."

"Right, thanks." Strong turned to the intercom mike, calling, "Captain Strong to control tower, check in."

"Say, I'd like to see this fellow blast," said Tom. "He's supposed to be one of the hottest pilots ever to hit space."

"Yeah," agreed Roger. "He's so good I don't see how anyone else could have a chance."

"With that hot rocket in this race," said Astro, "the others will have to fight for second and third place."

"Control tower to Strong," a voice crackled over the intercom loudspeaker. "Ready here, sir."

"Right. Stand by for the next flight, Mac," replied Strong. "It's Sticoon."

Strong flipped a switch on the intercom to direct contact with the waiting ship and gave Sticoon the oft-repeated final briefing, concluding, "Do not go beyond the necessary limitations of fuel consumption that are provided for in the Solar Guard space code. If you return here with less than a quarter supply of reactant fuel, you will be disqualified. Stand by to blast off!"

"Uh-huh!" was all the acknowledgment Strong received from the Martian. Famed for his daring, Sticoon was also known for his taciturn personality.

"Clear ramp! Clear ramp!" Strong boomed over the public-address system. When he received the all-clear from the enlisted spaceman on the ramp, Strong flipped both the public-address system and the intercom on. "Stand by to raise ship!"

He glanced at the astral chronometer. "Blast off, minus five, four, three, two, one— *zero!*"

Tom, Roger, and Astro crowded to the viewport in Strong's command shack to watch the bulky Martian's ship take to space. With Sticoon at the controls, there was no hesitation. He gave the ship full throttle from the moment of blast-off and in three seconds was out of sight. There wasn't much to see at such speed.

The three members of the *Polaris* unit left the shack to return to their task of inspection. They passed the maintenance hangar where Kit Barnard was readying his ship for blast-off in the next half hour.

"Any last-minute hitches, Kit?" asked Astro, vitally interested in the new reactor unit and its cooling system.

Kit smiled wearily and shook his head. "All set!"

"Good." Tom smiled. "We'll try to be back before you blast. We've got to check Quent Miles' ship now."

As the three cadets approached the sleek black vessel with its distinctive markings, the airlock opened and Quent Miles stepped out on the ladder.

"It's about time you three jerks showed up," he sneered. "I have to blast off in twenty minutes! What's the idea of messing around with that Barnard creep? He hasn't got a chance, anyway."

"Is that so?" snapped Roger. "Listen—!"

"Roger!" barked Tom warningly.

Quent grinned. "That's right. Lay off, buster. Get to your inspecting and let a spaceman blast off."

"Kit Barnard will blast off after you, and still beat you back," growled Roger, stepping into the ship. He stopped suddenly and gasped in amazement. "Well, blast my jets!"

Tom and Astro crowded into the airlock and looked

around, openmouthed. Before them was what appeared to be a hollow shell of a ship. There were no decks or bulkheads, nothing but an intricate network of ladders connecting the various operating positions of the spaceship. Everything that could be removed had been taken out of the ship.

"Is this legal?" asked Roger incredulously.

"I'm afraid it is, Roger," said Tom. "But we're going to make sure that everything that's supposed to be in a spaceship is in this one."

"When I blast off, I don't intend carrying any passengers," growled Miles behind them. "If you're going to inspect, then inspect and stop gabbing."

"Let's go," said Tom grimly.

The three boys split up and began crawling around in the network of exposed supporting beams and struts that took the place of decks and bulkheads. It did not take them long to determine that Quent Miles' ship was in perfect condition for blast-off. With but a few minutes to spare, they returned to face Miles at the airlock.

"OK, you're cleared," Tom announced.

"But it'll take more than a light ship to win this race," said Roger, and unable to restrain himself, he added, "You're bucking the best space busters in the universe!"

"One of them"—Quent held up his finger—"is dead."

"Yeah," growled Astro, "but there are plenty more just as good as Gigi Duarte."

The intercom buzzer sounded in the ship and Quent snapped, "Beat it! I've got a race to win." He pushed the three cadets out of the airlock and slammed the pluglike door closed. From two feet away it was impossible to spot the seams in the metal covering on the port and the hull.

"Clear ramp! Clear ramp!" Strong's voice echoed over the spaceport. Tom, Roger, and Astro scurried down the ladder and broke away from the ramp in a run. They knew Quent Miles would not hesitate to blast off whether anyone was within range of his exhaust or not.

"Blast off, minus five, four, three, two, one—*zero!*"

Again the spaceport reverberated to the sound of a ship blasting off. All eyes watched the weirdly painted black ship shudder under the surge of power, and then shoot spaceward as if out of a cannon.

"Well, ring me around Saturn," breathed Tom, looking up into the sky where the black ship had disappeared from view. "Whatever Quent Miles is, he can sure take acceleration."

"Spaceman," said Astro, taking a deep breath, "you can say that again. Wow!"

"I hope it broke his blasted neck," said Roger.

"AND YOU SAW HIM MESSING AROUND HERE, SID?" asked Kit Barnard of his young helper.

"That's right," replied the crew chief. "I was on the control deck checking out the panel and I happened to look down. I couldn't see too well, but it was a big guy."

"Messing around the reactor, huh?" mused Kit, almost asking the question of himself.

"That's right. I checked it right away, but I couldn't find anything wrong."

"Well, it's too late now, anyway. I blast in three minutes." Grimly Kit Barnard looked up at the sky where the black ship had just vanished.

"Spaceman's luck, Kit," said Sid, offering his hand. Kit grasped it quickly and jumped into his ship, closing the airlock behind him.

As Sid climbed down from the ramp, the three cadets rushed up breathlessly, disappointed at being unable to give Kit their personal good wishes.

"Well, anyway, I gave the new reactor my blessing last night," said Astro as they walked away from the ramp.

"You were aboard the ship last night?" Sid exclaimed.

"Uh-huh," replied Astro.

"Hope you don't mind."

"No, not a bit!" Sid broke into a smile. "Whew! I thought for a while it was Quent."

"What about Quent?" asked Tom.

"I saw someone messing around on the power deck last night and thought it might be Quent. But now that you say it was you, Astro, there isn't anything to worry about."

Reaching a safe distance from the ramp, they stopped just as Strong finished counting off the seconds to blast off.

"Zero!"

The three cadets and Sid waited for the initial shattering roar of the jets, but it did not come. Instead, there was a loud bang, followed by another, and then another. And only then did the ship begin to leave the ground, gradually picking up speed and shooting spaceward.

"What was wrong?" asked Tom, looking at Sid.

"The feeders," replied the young engineer miserably. "They're not functioning properly. They're probably jamming."

Astro looked puzzled. "But I checked those feeders myself, just before you closed the casing," he said. "They were all right then."

"Are you sure?" asked Sid.

"Of course I'm sure," said Astro. "Checking the feeders is one of my main jobs."

"Then it must be the reactant," said Tom. "Did Kit use standard reactant?"

Sid nodded. "Got it right here at the spaceport. Same stuff everyone else is using."

Gloomily the four young spacemen turned away from the ramp and headed for the control tower to hear the latest reports from the ships already underway. There were only a few more ships scheduled to blast off, and the cadets had already inspected them.

"Wait a minute," said Tom, stopping suddenly. "The fuel tanks are on the portside of the ship, and the feeders are on the starboard. Where did you see this fellow messing around, Sid?"

Sid thought a moment and then his face clouded. "Come to think of it, I saw him on the portside."

"I wasn't even close to the tanks!" exclaimed Astro.

"There was someone messing around them, then," said Roger.

"Yes," said Tom grimly. "But we don't know *who*—or *what* he did."

"From the sound of those rockets," said Astro, "Kit's feeders are clogged, or there's something in his reactant that the strainers are not filtering out."

"Well," sighed Roger, "there isn't anything Kit can do but keep going and hope that everything turns out for the best."

"*If* he can keep going!" said Tom. "You know, there are some things about this whole race that really puzzle me."

"What?" asked Roger.

"Impure reactant in Kit's ship, after fellows like Kit, Astro, and Sid checked it a hundred times. Gigi Duarte crashing after making record speed to the Moon. The minimum specifications being stolen from Commander Walters...." Tom stopped and looked at his friends. "That enough?"

Roger, Astro, and Sid considered the young cadet's words. The picture Tom presented had many curious sides and no one had the slightest idea of how to go beyond speculation and find proof!

6 "THE WINNERS ARE—" CAPTAIN STRONG'S VOICE RANG LOUD AND CLEAR OVER THE LOUDSPEAKERS—

"first place, Captain Sticoon, piloting the Marsopolis Limited entry, *Space Lance*! Second place, Captain Miles, piloting the Charles Brett Company entry, *Space Knight*! Third place, Captain Barnard, piloting his own ship, *Good Company*!"

There was a tremendous roar from the crowd. In front of the official stand, Tom, Roger, and Astro pounded Sid Goldberg on the back until he begged for mercy. On the stand, Strong and Kit shook hands and grinned at each other. And Commander Walters stepped up to congratulate the three winners. Walters handed each of them a personal message of good wishes from the Solar Council, and then, over the public-address system, made a short speech to the pilots of the losing ships thanking them for their cooperation and good sportsmanship. He paused, and in a voice hushed with emotion, offered a short prayer in memory of Gigi Duarte. The entire spaceport was quiet for two minutes without prompting, voluntarily paying homage to the brave spaceman.

After Walters left and the ceremonies were over, the three winners stood looking at each other, sizing up one another. Each of them knew that the winner of this race probably would go down in the history of deep space. There was fame and fortune to be won now. Quent Miles ignored Sticoon and swaggered over to Kit Barnard.

"You were lucky, Barnard," he sneered. "Too bad it won't last for the race."

"We'll see, Quent," said Kit coolly.

Sticoon said nothing, just watched them quietly. Quent Miles laughed and walked off the stand. Kit Barnard looked at Sticoon. "What's the matter with him?" he asked.

The Martian shrugged. "Got a hot rocket in his craw," he said quietly. "But watch your step with him, Kit. Personally, I wouldn't trust that spaceman as far as I could throw an asteroid."

Kit grinned. "Thanks—and good luck."

"I'll need it if you get that reactor of yours working," said the Martian.

He turned and left the stand without a word to Tom, Roger, or Astro. The three cadets looked at each other, feeling the tension in the air suddenly relax. Strong was busy talking to someone on the portable intercom and had missed the byplay between the three finalists.

"That Quent sure has a talent for making himself disliked," Tom commented to his unit mates.

"And all he's going to get for it is trouble," quipped Sid, who would not let any argument take away the pleasure he felt over winning the trials. "I'm going back to our ship and find out what happened to those feeders."

"I'll come with you," volunteered Astro.

"Just a minute, Astro," interrupted Strong. "I've been talking with Commander Walters. He's on his way back to the Tower of Galileo and called me from the portable communicator on the main slidewalk. He wants me to report to his office on the double. You three will have to take care of the final details here."

"Come down when you can," said Sid to Astro, and turned to leave with Kit.

"Something wrong, sir?" asked Tom.

"I don't know, Tom," replied Strong, a worried frown on his face. "Commander Walters seemed excited."

"Does it have anything to do with the race?" asked Roger.

"In a way it does," replied Strong. "I'm leaving on special assignment. I'm not sure, but I think you three will have to monitor the race by yourselves."

MAJOR CONNEL SAT TO ONE SIDE of Commander Walters' desk, a scowl on his heavy, fleshy face. The commander paced back and forth in front of the desk, and Captain Strong stood at the office window staring blankly down on the dark quadrangle below. The door opened and the three officers turned quickly to see Dr. Joan Dale enter, carrying several papers in her hand.

"Well, Joan?" asked Walters.

"I'm afraid that the reports are true, sir," Dr. Dale said. "There are positive signs of decreasing pressure in the artificial atmosphere around the settlements on Titan. The pressure is dropping and yet there is no indication that the force screen, holding back the real methane ammonia atmosphere of Titan, is not functioning properly."

"How about leaks?" Connel growled.

"Not possible, Major," replied the pretty physicist. "The force field, as you know, is made up of electronic impulses of pure energy. By shooting these impulses into the air around a certain area, like the settlement at Olympia, we can refract the methane ammonia, push it back if you will, like a solid wall. What the impulses do, actually, is create a force greater and thicker in content than the atmosphere of Titan, creating a vacuum. We then introduce oxygen into the vacuum, making it possible for humans to live without the cumbersome use of space helmets." Dr. Dale leaned against Commander Walters' desk and considered the three Solar Guard officers. "If we don't find out what's happening out there," she resumed grimly, "and do something about it soon, we'll have to abandon Titan."

"Abandon Titan!" roared Connel. "Can't be done."

"Impossible!" snapped Walters.

"It's going to happen," asserted the girl stoutly.

Connel sprang out of his chair and began pacing the floor. "We can't abandon Titan!" he roared. "Disrupt the flow of crystal and you'll set off major repercussions in the system's economy."

"We know that, Major," said Walters. "That's the prime reason for this meeting."

"May I make a suggestion, sir?" asked Strong.

"Go ahead, Steve," said Walters.

"While these graphs of Joan's show us *what's* happening, I think it will take on-the-spot investigations to find out *why* it's happening."

Connel flopped back in his chair, relaxed again. He looked at Walters. "Send Steve out there and we'll find out what's going on," he said confidently.

Walters looked at Strong. "When are the ships supposed to blast off for the race?"

"Tomorrow at 1800, sir."

"You planned to use the *Polaris* to monitor the race?"

"Yes, sir."

"Think we should send the *Polaris* unit out alone?"

"I have a better suggestion, sir," said Strong.

"Well?"

"Since there are only three finalists, how about putting one cadet on each ship? Then I can take the *Polaris* and go on out to Titan now. When the boys arrive, they could help me with my investigation."

Walters looked at Connel. "What do you think, Major?"

"Sounds all right to me," replied the veteran spaceman. "If you think the companies won't object to having cadets monitor their race for them."

"They won't have anything to say about it," replied Walters. "I'd trust those cadets under any circumstances. And the race won't mean a thing unless we can find the source of trouble on Titan. There won't be any crystal to haul."

"Fine," grunted Connel. He rose, nodded, and left the room. He was not being curt, he was being Connel. The problem had been temporarily solved and there was nothing else he could do. There were other things that demanded his attention.

"What about me going along too, Commander?" asked Joan.

"Better not, Joan," said Walters. "You're more valuable to us here in the Academy laboratory."

"Very well, sir," she said. "I have some work to finish, so I'll leave you now. Good luck, Steve." She shook hands with the young captain and left.

Walters turned back to Strong. "Well, now that's settled, tell me, what do you think of the race tomorrow, Steve?"

"If Kit Barnard gets that reactor of his functioning properly, he'll run away from the other two."

"I don't know," mused Walters. "Wild Bill Sticoon is a hot spaceman. One of the best rocket jockeys I've ever seen. Did I ever tell you what we went through a few years back trying to get him to join the Solar Guard?" Walters laughed. "We promised him everything but the Moon. But he didn't want any part of us. 'Can't ride fast enough in your wagons, Commander,' he told me. Quite a boy!"

"And with Quent Miles in there, it's going to be a very hot race," asserted Strong.

"Ummmmh," Walters grunted. "He's the unknown quantity. Did you see that ship of his? Never saw anything more streamlined in my whole life."

"And the cadets said he stripped her of everything but the hull plates."

"It paid off for him," said Walters. "He and Charley Brett are certainly working hard to get this contract."

"There's a lot of money involved, sir," said Strong. "But in any case, we're bound to get a good schedule with the speeds established so far."

"Well, advise the cadets to stand by for blast-off with the finalists tomorrow."

"Any particular ship you want them each assigned to,

sir?" asked Strong.

"No, let them decide," replied Walters. "But it would be best if you could keep Manning away from Miles. That's like putting a rocket into a fire and asking it not to explode."

The two men grinned at each other and then settled down to working out the details of Strong's trip. Before the evening was over, Walters had decided, if necessary, he would follow Strong out to Titan.

In the distance, they could hear the muffled roar of rocket motors as the three finalists tuned up their ships, preparing for the greatest space race in history. And it seemed to Strong that with each blast there was a vaguely ominous echo.

"I'VE STRAINED THAT FUEL FOUR times and come up with the same answer," said Astro. The giant Venusian held up the oil-smeared test tube for Kit Barnard's inspection. "Impure reactant. And so impure that it couldn't possibly have come from the Academy supply depot. It would have been noticed."

"Then how did it get in my feeders?" asked Kit, half to himself.

"Whoever was messing around on the power deck just before you blasted off for the trials must have dumped it in," said Tom.

"Obviously." Kit nodded. "But who is that? Who would want to do a dirty thing like that?"

"Who indeed?" said a voice in back of them. They all spun around to face Quent Miles. He lounged against the stabilizer fin and grinned at them.

"What do you want, Miles?" asked Kit.

"Just stopped by to give you the proverbial handshake of good luck before we blast off," replied the spaceman with a mocking wink.

"Kit doesn't need your good wishes," snapped Sid.

"Well, now, that's too bad," said Quent. "I have a feeling that he's going to need a lot more than luck."

"Listen, Miles," snapped Kit, "did you come aboard my ship and tamper with the fuel?"

Quent's eyes clouded. "Careful of your accusations, Barnard."

"I'm not accusing you, I'm asking you."

"See you in space." Quent laughed, turning to leave, not answering the question. "But then, again, maybe I won't see you." He disappeared into the darkness of the night.

"The nerve of that guy," growled Tom.

"Yes," Kit agreed, shrugging his shoulders. "But I'm more concerned about this unit than I am about Quent Miles and his threats. Let's get back to work."

Renewing their efforts, Tom, Roger, Astro, Sid, and Kit Barnard turned to the reactor unit and began the laborious job of putting it back together again, at the same time replacing worn-out parts and adjusting the delicate clearances.

It was just before dawn when Strong visited Kit's ship. Seeing the cadets stripped to the waist and working with the veteran spaceman, he roared his disapproval. "Of all the crazy things to do! Don't you know that you could have Kit disqualified for helping him?"

"But—but—" Tom tried to stammer an explanation.

"I couldn't have done it alone," explained Kit. He looked at Strong and their eyes met. Understanding flowed between them.

"Very well," said Strong, fighting to control himself. "If no one makes a complaint against you, we'll let it pass."

"Thanks, Steve," said Kit.

"You should have known better, Kit," said Strong. "The Solar Guard is supposed to be neutral throughout the entire race and do nothing but judge it."

"I know, Steve," said Kit. "But someone dumped impure reactant into my—"

"What?" It was the first time Strong had heard of it and

he listened intently as the cadets and Sid told him the whole story.

"Why didn't you make a complaint?" demanded Strong finally. "We'd have given you more time to get squared away."

"It's not important," said Kit. "I won a place in the finals and now the boys and Sid have helped me clean it out."

Strong nodded. "All right. I guess one seems to balance out the other. Forget it." He smiled. "And excuse me for jumping like that and thinking that you would do any-thing—er—" He hesitated.

"That's all right, Steve." Kit spoke up quickly to save his friend embarrassment.

Strong turned to the cadets. "I've got news for you three. You are going to monitor the race by yourselves."

Tom, Roger, and Astro looked at each other dumfounded as Strong quickly outlined the plan. Later, when Sid and Kit were working inside the ship, he told them of the sudden danger on Titan.

"So I'm going to leave it up to you which ship you want to ride," he concluded. "The commander has suggested that Roger not be sent along with Miles on the *Space Knight*. He seems to think the two of you wouldn't get along."

"On the contrary, skipper," said Roger, "I'd like the op-portunity of keeping an eye on him."

Strong thought a moment. "Not a bad idea, Roger," he said as he turned to Astro. "And I suppose you want to ride with Kit and his reactor?"

Astro grinned. "Yes, sir. If I may."

"All right. Tom, I guess that means you ride with Wild Bill Sticoon."

"That's all right with me, sir," the young cadet said ex-citedly. "This is something I'll be able to tell my grandchil-dren—riding with the hottest spaceman in the hottest race through space."

QUENT MILES SPUN AROUND, his paralo-ray gun leveled. He saw a figure enter through the hatch, but when light re-vealed the face he relaxed.

"Oh, it's you!" he grumbled. "I thought you were setting

things up back at Atom City."

"You fumble-fisted, space-gassing jerk!" snarled Charley Brett. "Depend on you to get things messed up! That Barnard guy is all set to roll with his reactor!"

"Then why didn't Ross take care of him on the Moon?" asked Miles.

"He didn't land," replied Brett. "He kept going and made the whole trip without refueling that new unit of his. It's so good that he got back here still carrying half a tank of reactant."

"Well, you haven't any kick with me," asserted Miles. "I dumped that stuff in his tanks."

"Then how come he made it so fast?" growled Brett. "How come he made it at all?"

"How should I know?" snapped Quent. "Listen, Charley, lay off me. You might be able to order Ross around, but you don't scare me. And I don't think you have Ross fooled either."

"Never mind that now!" said Brett irritably. "We've got to line things up for the race. Listen! Ross left Luna City this morning for the hideout. Here's what I want you to do. After you blast off—" Brett's voice dropped to a whisper and Quent's eyes opened with understanding, and then his rugged features broke out into a grin as Brett continued talking.

Finally Brett straightened up. "I'm going on out to Titan now to see if things are OK. You got everything clear?"

"Everything's clear," said Quent. "And you know something, Charley? You have a nasty way about you, but you certainly know how to figure the angles. This is perfect. We can't miss."

"I love you too, sweetheart," said Brett sourly. He turned and hurried out of the ship. Just before he stepped on the slidewalk that would take him to the monorail station, he saw the three members of the *Polaris* unit leaving Kit Barnard's installation. He grinned and made a mocking salute to them in the darkness.

"So long suckers!" he called softly.

7 "WHAT!" QUENT MILES LOOKED AT STRONG AND THEN BACK AT ROGER. "YOU MEAN THIS JERK'S GOING TO RIDE WITH ME?"

Roger Manning squared his shoulders and stuck out his chin. "Let's make the most of this, Miles," he said. "I don't like it any more than you do. I wouldn't like to be watched, either, if I had just crawled out from under a rock."

Strong suppressed a grin and then turned back to Quent. "That's the way it is, Miles. Commander Walters' orders. There's nothing that can be done now. Cadets Manning, Corbett, and Astro have been given these assignments because they have worked so closely on the race project, and, I might add, you couldn't ask for a better astrogator should you get into trouble."

"The day I'll ask for help from a kid still wet behind the ears is the day I'll stop flying," snarled Miles.

Strong shrugged. "You either consent to the regulations or disqualify yourself from the race."

The spaceman's face turned a dusky red under his swarthy complexion. "All right, all right! If that's the way it is, that's the way we'll play it. But I'm warning you, Manning, stay away from me."

Strong glanced at his wrist chronograph. "You have five minutes before the blast-off, stand by." He shook hands with Roger. "Good luck, Roger, and be careful. And remember, Captain Miles has already proved himself a crackerjack spaceman. Don't interfere with him."

"Yes, sir," said Roger.

"Good luck, Miles," said Strong and offered his hand. Quent ignored it.

"Thanks for nothing," he sneered. "I know how much you want me to have."

"The best man wins," snapped Strong. He turned on his heels and left the black ship.

Quent Miles and Roger faced each other. "All right, Manning," said Miles after he had closed the airlock, "take your station. And remember I'm skipper of this ship."

"So what?" said Roger. "I'm still the monitor—!" He turned and swaggered away.

Miles watched him go, a crooked smile twisting his lips. "Make the most of it, Manning," he muttered under his breath.

"You WILL MAKE TWO STOPS for refueling on your trip," Captain Strong called over the loudspeakers, as well as into the intercom connecting the three ships. "First fuel stop will be on Deimos of Mars and the second will be at Ganymede. You are to chart a direct course to each of them. Should an emergency arise, you will call for assistance on the special teleceiver and audioceiver circuits open to you, numbers seventeen and eighty-three. You are to circle each fueling stop three times before making a touchdown, and make a final circle around Titan when you arrive.

"Stand by to raise ship! And spaceman's luck!"

Strong turned and flipped on the intercom to the control tower. "All ready up there?" he called.

"All set, sir," replied the enlisted spaceman.

"All right, give them their orbits and blast-off time."

There was a slight pause, and then the gruff voice of the tower operator was heard over the loudspeakers and in the ships. "All ships will blast off on orbit forty-one ... raise ship at 18:51:35 ... stand by!"

There was a tense moment of silence while the seconds on the red hand of the astral chronometer slipped around the dial. Out on the field, the three ships were pointed toward the darkening afternoon skies. The first ship, nearest the tower, was Wild Bill Sticoon's ship, the *Space Lance*, painted a gleaming white. Strong could see Tom sitting beside the viewport, and across the distance that separated them, the Solar Guard officer could see the curly-haired cadet wave. He returned the greeting.

Next was the black ship with the red markings that had aroused so much comment. Strong searched the viewports for a sight of Roger but could not see him. Finally, he looked over at Kit Barnard's red-painted *Good Company.* He knew Astro would be on the power deck, preferring to nurse the reactor than watch the blast-off.

And then Strong was conscious of the tower operator counting off the seconds. He would pick it up at ten minus. Strong gripped the intercom mike as the voice droned in his ears.

"...fifteen, fourteen, thirteen, twelve, eleven, ten...."

"Stand by to raise ships!" bawled Strong. He watched the sweep hand on the chronometer. "Blast off, minus five, four, three, two, one— *zero!*"

There was really very little to see. The three ships left Earth in a giant upheaval of thunderous noise and blazing red exhaust flames. The roar of the crowds was lost in the explosions of the rockets. And the greatest race in space was underway.

Strong raced up to the control tower and stood in front of the radar scanner to watch the course of the three vessels now blasting through the atmosphere. They were three white blips on the green surface of the glass scope, in per-fect line, traveling at incredible speeds.

Strong turned to the enlisted spaceman. "Contact the ships and see if everything's all right," he ordered.

"Very well, sir," replied the spaceman, turning to the au-dioceiver microphone.

"Spaceport control to rocket ships *Space Lance, Space Knight,* and *Good Company.* Come in, please."

There was a crackling of static over the loudspeaker and then the calm voice of Tom filled the control tower. "This is Corbett on the *Space Lance.* Go ahead."

Strong took the microphone. "This is Captain Strong," he called. "How was your blast-off, Tom?"

"Smooth as silk, sir," replied the young cadet. "Wild Bill sends his greetings and says he'll take a three-inch steak instead of flowers when he wins."

"Tell him it's a deal." Strong laughed. "End transmission."

"See you on Titan, sir," said Tom. "End transmission."

Strong then spoke to Kit Barnard on the *Good Company,* but did not get a chance to speak to Astro. "He's down on the power deck, Steve," reported Kit. "He's watching that reactor as if it were a treasure chest."

"To him it *is*," said Strong. "Good luck, Kit."

"Incidentally," said Kit before signing off, "I heard that crack Wild Bill made about a steak. Better put *my* name on it!"

Strong then contacted Quent Miles' vessel. "Is Manning there, Miles?"

"Yeah, he's here. Dead asleep!" growled Miles. "I thought you said he was going to be a help."

Strong's face grew red. "Well, wake him up," he snapped.

"You come wake him up," said Miles, and then the speaker went dead.

"Control tower to *Space Knight!*" Strong called angrily. "Come in, Miles. Control tower to *Space Knight!*"

"Yeah. What do you want?" growled Miles over the vast distance of space that already separated the two men and that each second took them thousands of miles farther apart.

"I want to speak to Manning," demanded Strong. "And if you cut me off like that again, Miles, I'll have you before a Solar Guard court for violation of the space code, race or no race."

"I told you once," said Miles. "Manning is asleep. He sacked in right after we left the Academy. Now leave me alone, will you! I've got a race to win!"

"Very well, Miles," said Strong. "But for your sake, I hope Cadet Manning *is* asleep."

"End transmission," growled Miles, and again the speaker went dead.

"Trouble, Steve?"

Strong turned to see Commander Walters enter the control room.

"No, sir," said Strong. "I tried to contact Roger, but Quent Miles told me he's asleep."

"Asleep!" cried Walters. "But I thought you weren't going to put Manning with Miles."

"Astro wanted to go with Kit, sir. And Tom was anxious to go with Wild Bill Sticoon. Roger didn't seem to mind."

"Did Miles object?"

"Yes, sir. But I think he would object to anyone going

with him."

"And he told you Roger is asleep?"

Strong nodded. Walters pushed past him to the intercom and took the microphone. "This is Commander Walters calling rocket ship *Space Knight*. Come in, *Space Knight*."

There was a flutter of static and then Quent Miles' voice again. There was a little more respect in his tone but his story was the same. Roger was sleeping.

Walters slammed the microphone down. "By the craters of Luna, this is the last time I'll take this nonsense from Manning!" He jerked around and stood facing the viewport. "I'm sorry, Steve, but there have been more reports from Titan. The situation is serious.

I've had to start evacuation. And then to get this smart-alecky behavior out of Manning. Well, you know what I mean."

Strong nodded, now more concerned about the emergency on Mars. "Shall I blast off right away, sir?" he asked.

Walters nodded grimly. "Yes. And I'm going with you. I'll leave Major Connel in charge while I'm gone. I would prefer to have him go, but he's been working with Dr. Dale on some new idea about reinforcing the force field and I can't pull him off it. You and I will have to do what we can."

Strong turned to the tower operator and ordered the rocket cruiser *Polaris* readied for immediate space flight, concluding, "...And have a full complement of Space Marines aboard. And I want Warrant Officer Mike McKenny as squad leader."

"Have you forgotten, sir?" interjected the enlisted spaceman who was taking Strong's orders. "Warrant Officer McKenny cannot take acceleration."[4]

"All right, get—" Strong hesitated. "Get me Jeff Marshall, Professor Sykes' assistant."

Walters nodded. "Good idea. Jeff can take care of any lab tests we may have to make and also knows how to handle men. As a matter of fact," Walters continued, "if Jeff does

---

[4] Tough guy McKenny drilled three raw recruits—Tom, Roger and Astro—in *Stand By For Mars!* He last appeared in book 4, *The Space Pioneers,* but the physical limitation grounding the warrant officer is not mentioned.

well on this assignment I might put him up for a commission in the Solar Guard. He did well on that last trip into deep space during that trouble on Roald."[5]

"Yes, sir," said Strong. "And I'll gladly endorse it."

"Is that all, sir?" asked the enlisted man.

"That's it, spaceman!" said Strong. When the man didn't move right away, Walters and Strong looked at him. "Well, what is it?"

"Excuse me, sir," said the guardsman, a bright-faced youngster who had failed to pass the rigid requirements for cadet training and so had entered the enlisted Solar Guard. "I heard what Captain Miles said about Cadet Manning being asleep and—" He hesitated.

"Well, what about it?" prompted Walters.

"Well, sir, I don't know if it means anything or not," replied the boy nervously. "But just before the ship blasted off, I saw Cadet Manning standing inside the airlock. He looked as if he wanted to get out. But you were counting the blast-off time, sir. And he disappeared a few seconds before you hit zero."

Strong looked at Walters. "Are you sure?" he asked the boy.

"I'm positive, sir. I know Cadet Manning well, and he looked as though he was scared."

Strong clenched his fists. "Asleep, huh?" he growled. "Get me the *Space Knight!*"

The boy returned to the audioceiver and began calling Miles, but there was no reply. After a few minutes Walters interrupted, "We can't waste any more time here, Steve. We've got to blast off!"

"Get hold of Corbett on the *Space Lance*," said Strong to the spaceman. "Tell him I said to get in touch with Manning on the *Space Knight*. Ask him to find out what's going on."

"Yes, sir."

"And then tell him to contact me on the *Polaris*. We're

---

[5] In *The Space Pioneers,* Roald is "a newly discovered satellite in orbit around the sun star Wolf 359" —thirteen light years from earth. Roald also harbors an enigmatic force that causes approaching shapeships to crash.

blasting off immediately."

"Very well, sir."

Walters turned to Captain Strong. "What do you think it means, Steve?" he asked.

"I can't figure it, sir. Knowing Manning as I do, it could be a crazy stunt or it could be serious."

"It had better be serious," said Walters grimly, "for Manning's sake. One more slip, and I'm bouncing him right out of the Academy!"

The two officers left the control tower, leaving young Oliver Muffin alone, droning his monotonous call to Tom Corbett, somewhere between Earth and Mars—a call that was to be the young cadet's first warning of treachery in deep space!

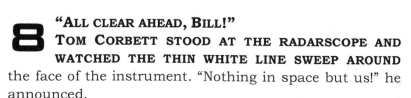

8 "ALL CLEAR AHEAD, BILL!" TOM CORBETT STOOD AT THE RADARSCOPE AND WATCHED THE THIN WHITE LINE SWEEP AROUND the face of the instrument. "Nothing in space but us!" he announced.

The veteran spaceman grunted and grinned at the curly-haired cadet he had grown to like and respect in the short time they had been together. Not only did Tom know how to handle a ship, spelling the pilot for a few moments to have a walk around the control deck, but he was good company as well. More than once, Tom had surprised the Martian spaceman with his sober judgment of the minor decisions Sticoon had to make in flight.

"Why don't you try to contact Manning again, Tom?" Sticoon suggested. "He might be awake now."

Tom grinned, but in his heart he did not think it very funny. It was no joke that Captain Strong had called him to contact Roger. And Tom was worried. So far, he had not been able to reach the blond-haired cadet. He settled himself in front of the communicator and began calling the black ship again.

"Rocket ship *Space Lance* to rocket ship *Space Knight*! Come in!"

He waited. Nothing but static and silence greeted him.

"*Space Knight*, come in!"

He waited again as the sleek white ship plummeted deeper into space toward the first refueling stop on Deimos, one of the small twin moons of Mars. Still there was no acknowledging reply from the black ship that had streaked ahead of them after the blast-off.

"I'm going to try to contact Kit Barnard," said Tom. "Maybe he can pick up Miles' blip on his radar."

Tom made the necessary adjustment on the audioceiver and broadcast the call for the owner-pilot of the *Good Company*. Finally, after repeated tries, he heard a faint signal and recognized the voice of his unit mate Astro.

"What's the matter, Astro?" asked Tom. "I can hardly hear you."

"We're having trouble with the bypass lines to the generators," replied Astro. "We've cut down to standard space speed, and Sid and Kit are making repairs now."

"Have you heard from Roger?" asked Tom across the vast abyss of space separating them. "I've been trying to contact the *Space Knight* for the last six hours and can't get any acknowledgment."

"Haven't seen it," replied Astro. "Lost contact with her a long time ago. She moved ahead at emergency space speed and we lost her on our radar an hour after we blasted off."

"OK, Astro. Hope Kit gets his wagon going again. We've got to make a race of this, or the people throughout the system will be disappointed." He turned and winked at Wild Bill.

"Listen, you curly-haired twerp!" roared Astro, and it seemed to Tom that he could hear his friend without the loudspeaker. "We're going to give you the hottest run of your lives when we get going!" ·

"OK, Astro," said Tom. "If you can contact Roger, tell him to get in touch with Captain Strong right away. He's probably blasted off on the *Polaris* by now."

"Right, Tom. End transmission."

"End transmission."

Tom turned back to the skipper of the *Space Lance* with a feeling of despair. "I can't figure it out, Bill," he said. "Roger's pulled some boners before, real rocket blasters, but refusing to answer a call from Strong—" He shook his head.

The audioceiver suddenly crackled into life. "*Space Knight* to *Space Lance*, check in!" Quent Miles' voice was harsh and clear.

Tom jumped back to the microphone. "*Space Lance*, Cadet Corbett here!" he shouted eagerly. "Go ahead, *Space Knight*! Where's Manning?"

"Still asleep!" replied Miles. "Just wanted to tell you boys good-by. I'm not stopping to refuel at Deimos! I'm going right on through to Ganymede! End transmission!"

Only static filled the control deck of the *Space Lance* as Tom clutched the microphone and pleaded desperately for Quent Miles to answer him. "Come in, Miles! This is Corbett on the *Space Lance* to Quent Miles on the *Space Knight*! Come in, Miles! Come in!"

Bill Sticoon shook his head. "Miles must be nuts trying to get to Ganymede without refueling," he muttered. "Traveling at emergency space speed, he'll eat up his fuel before he gets one third of the way to Jupiter!"

Tom looked at Sticoon. "And Roger's with him."

Sticoon nodded grimly. "They'll wind up drifting around in space halfway between Mars and Jupiter. Finding them will be about as easy as looking for a pebble in the Martian desert."

"HAVE YOU FOUND THE *SPACE LANCE* YET, ASTRO?" asked Kit Barnard, glancing over his shoulder at the giant Venusian, standing at the radarscope.

"I think I'm getting it now," said Astro. "Either that or I've picked up an asteroid."

"Not likely," said Kit. "We're too far from the belt to have anything that big drifting around without being charted. It must be Sticoon."

"Boy!" chuckled Astro. "This reactor really packs a load of power!"

"How are we doing on fuel, Sid?" Kit called into the intercom.

"We lost a lot trying to prime the pumps," replied the young crew chief. "We have to touch down on Deimos and refuel."

"That's all right," replied Kit with a smile. "We're gaining on Sticoon fast. We should make Deimos about the same time. I wonder where Quent Miles is by now."

"Probably wishing he had stopped for fuel!" interjected Astro with a sour look on his face.

"See if you can pick up Sticoon on the audioceiver, Astro," said Kit. "Ask him for an estimated time of arrival on Deimos. One of us will have to come in first."

Astro flipped the switch on the panel and began his call "*Good Company* to *Space Lance*, come in!"

"Right here, Astro," replied Tom immediately. "Boy, you certainly are burning up space! What have you got in your fuel tanks? Light speed?"

"Just a little thing we whipped up," said Astro with a grin. "What is your ETA on Deimos, Tom?"

"Less than five minutes. Four minutes and thirty seconds, to be exact. Think you can beat that?"

"If we can't beat it, we can equal it!" said Astro. "See you on the Martian moon, buddy! End transmission!"

Steadily, the *Good Company* rocketed through space, eating up the miles and gaining on the *Space Lance*. Both ships now made contact with the control tower on Deimos and received landing instructions.

"*Space Lance* will touch down on Ramp Three, *Good Company* on Ramp Six," crackled the voice of the Deimos tower operator, "and don't forget your approach orbits!"

"Have you heard from the *Space Knight*?" called Tom.

"Sorry, *Space Lance*," came the reply, "there has been no contact with *Space Knight*."

Tom began to feel the fingers of fear creeping up and down his spine. Quent Miles had carried out his plan of going on to Ganymede without refueling, threatening not only his own life, but Roger's as well.

Sticoon completed the three circling passes around Deimos and shouted to Tom over his shoulder. "Stand by,

Corbett. We're ready to go in!"

Tom strapped himself into his acceleration chair and, watching the atmospheric altimeter, a delicate instrument that recorded their height above the surface of a heavenly body, began to call off the indicated figures.

"Five thousand feet, four, three—dropping too fast—compensate for lesser gravity—two thousand, one, five hundred, two hundred—" Tom braced himself and seconds later felt the impact of the ship settling stern first on the concrete ramp. "Touchdown," he sang out in a clear voice.

While Sticoon secured the control deck, closing the many switches and circuits on the master panel, Tom opened the airlock. Almost immediately, specially trained crews swarmed into the ship to refuel her and prepare her for the next lap of the race. Tom and Sticoon stepped out onto the spaceport of the tiny moon of Mars and gazed up at the red planet that loomed large over the horizon. As a transfer point for the great passenger liners that rocketed between Venusport, Atom City, and Marsopolis, the refueling station at Deimos was well staffed and expertly manned.

Standing at the airlock, Tom and Sticoon heard the blasting roar of the *Good Company* coming down in a fast, expert touchdown, and they hurried across the spaceport to greet their rivals.

When the airlock opened, Tom immediately began to kid Astro and Sid, while Sticoon and Kit Barnard compared flight notes. A Universal Stereo reporter rushed up with a small portable camera and conducted an interview that was to be telecast back to Earth. Both spacemen were reluctant to voice any predictions of the outcome of the race, but Tom noticed that Kit was smiling and seemed in good spirits. Tom, with all his worries about Roger, could not help but feel happy that the independent spaceman was proving his reactor.

A man in the uniform of a Solar Guard major appeared. He introduced himself as an official monitor of the race, appointed by Commander Walters, and asked them for a report.

"Captain Sticoon has followed all regulations, sir," said Tom.

"And Captain Barnard, Cadet Astro?" asked the officer.

"Same thing, sir," replied Astro. "Captain Barnard has

followed the rules of the race exactly."

"Thank you," replied the officer and started to turn away.

"Any word from the *Space Knight*, sir?" Tom asked quickly.

"Nothing, Corbett," the officer replied. "We received the same message that Captain Miles would attempt to go on through to Ganymede without stopping here at Deimos for refueling."

"And you've heard nothing from him since, sir?" asked Astro.

"Nothing, why?" The officer looked at both of the boys sharply. "Anything wrong?"

"No, sir," said Tom. "It's just that Cadet Roger Manning is monitor on the *Space Knight* and we haven't been able to talk to him since we blasted off from Space Academy."

"I wouldn't worry about it if I were you, Cadet Corbett," snapped the major. "I've heard of Cadet Manning's reluctance to stick to regulations. I suspect you will be hearing from him soon enough, when the ship runs out of fuel and starts drifting around in the asteroid belt. Those individualists always scream for help when they get in trouble."

"Yes, sir," said Tom stiffly.

"I already have a squadron of ships standing by to go to their assistance when they do send out a distress alert."

"Yes, sir," said Tom. "Will that be all, sir? Cadet Astro and I would like to have a bite to eat before we blast off again."

"Yes, that will be all, Corbett. Don't wander off too far." The major turned and walked toward the ships without another word.

"Wonder what's eating him?" said Tom.

"Never mind," said Astro. "Come on. Let's grab a bite while we have the chance."

They headed for the restaurant in the control building of the spaceport but were recognized by the reporter of the stereo company who badgered them into stepping before the camera and making statements about the race. He tried to get the boys to commit themselves as to who they hoped would win, and to offer an opinion on what had happened to the *Space Knight*. But neither Tom nor Astro said anything but that the best man would win. There were the usual eager spectators too, thousands from the large cities on Mars who had taken the ferry rocket up to the spaceport to see the ships come in for refueling. As soon as Tom and Astro could tear away from the stereo reporter, they were mobbed by the onlookers who clamored for autographs. Finally the two cadets had to forego their meal and return to their respective ships to escape the wild demonstration.

Seated in his acceleration chair on the control deck of the *Space Lance*, waiting for Bill Sticoon to come aboard, Tom found his concern for Roger overriding his enthusiasm for the race. When Sticoon appeared and began to prepare the ship for blast-off, Tom went through the motions mechanically. The *Space Lance* was scheduled to leave first, with Kit Barnard following at the exact time interval of their arrivals. The Deimos tower operator's voice droned over the loudspeaker on the control deck of the *Space Lance* "...minus five, four, three, two, one"—then the breathtaking pause before the climactic— *"zero!"*

The ship shot spaceward, rockets roaring loudly in the thin atmosphere of the small satellite. The next moment, before the horrified eyes of thousands of people, the *Space Lance* exploded a few miles above the ground.

Astro stood frozen at the viewport of the *Good Company*, his eyes glazed with shock as he watched the Martian ship disintegrate far above him. All he could do was mutter brokenly, "Tom ... Tom...."

9

"BLAST OFF!" WITHOUT ANY PRELIMINARIES, KIT BAR-
NARD'S ORDER SENT THE *GOOD COMPANY* HURTLING
SPACEWARD. Astro had just enough time to throw
himself into an acceleration chair before the ship shot away
from the Deimos spaceport toward the wreckage of the
Space Lance.

"Braking rockets!" roared Kit. "Hit them hard, Sid."

The ship bucked under the force of the counter-acceler-
ation, and the veteran spaceman fought to keep her under
control. He snapped out another order. "Cut all rockets!"

The ship was suddenly quiet, hanging motionless in
space in the middle of the still-twisting wreckage. The huge
bank of atomic motors, the largest single unit on the ship,
had already begun to swing around the small moon Deimos
in an orbit, while other shattered remains of the once sleek
ship began a slow circle around the motors themselves.

Astro was struggling into a space suit when Sid and Kit
joined him in the airlock. Quickly the three spacemen
clamped their space helmets closed and adjusted the oxygen nozzles. Then, after testing their suit intercoms, they
closed the inner-portal airlock, reduced the air pressure,
and opened the thick pluglike outer portal. They stared out
at the gruesome spectacle of torn hull plates, twisted spars,
and broken pieces of equipment floating gently in velvet
space, outlined against the reddish hue of the planet Mars.

"Astro! Kit!" shouted Sid through the suit intercom.
"Look, there's Sticoon! Over there near that tube." Following
Sid's pointing finger, Astro and Kit turned toward an exhaust tube that
had been ripped in
half by the explo-
sion. The Martian
spaceman's body
floated next to it,
limp and broken.
Astro shuddered. If
Sticoon was dead,
then there was lit-
tle hope for Tom.
The big Venusian

fought back tears.

Maneuvering themselves away from the ship with the aid of the small jet packs strapped to their shoulders, they reached the dead spaceman. Sid carried him back to the ship while Astro and Kit remained to search the wreckage for Tom.

By now, three small jet boats and two rocket scouts had blasted off from Deimos, bringing emergency rescue equipment. More than a dozen men poured out of the ships and joined in the search. The work was carried on in silence. No one spoke.

Astro and Kit worked side by side, pushing their way gently through the twisting mass that was once a proud spaceship, to the heart of the spiraling wreckage, down toward the bank of atomic motors that was attracting all the lesser pieces. Suddenly Astro paled. He gripped the veteran's arm and gestured toward a large section of the ship on the other side of the motors that they had not seen before.

"By the stars," Kit gasped, "it's the airlock! All in one piece!"

"If Tom managed to get in there, or if he was in there when the ship exploded, maybe he has a chance."

"You're right, Astro," said Kit hopefully.

"But we can't open it out here," said Astro. "If Tom is inside, we have to take it down to Deimos. If we open it here, and he doesn't have a space suit on, he'd suffocate."

"He'd freeze solid before that," said Kit, not mentioning

the possibility that Tom might very well be frozen already, since the ship's heating units had been torn away from the airlock.

Quickly Astro hailed the members of the emergency crews that had rocketed up from Deimos and told them of the possibility that Tom was inside the chamber. They all agreed, since they had failed to find the cadet anywhere.

Kit and Astro immediately took charge of getting the bulky boxlike chamber back to Deimos where it could be opened safely. Two of the jet boats were jockeyed into position on either side of the chamber and several lengths of cable were stretched between them, forming a cradle for the chamber. Since the jet boats were equipped with foldaway wings, which, when extended, would enable them to fly at slower speed through atmosphere, they hoped to make a glider landing at the Deimos spaceport.

Astro would not let anyone handle the boats but Kit and himself, and only by threat of physical violence was he able to keep the regular pilots out of the control chairs on the speedy little ships. He might suffer for it later when the officers reported his actions, but the big Venusian was beyond caring. If Tom was not safe inside the vacuum chamber, he felt there wasn't much use in being a cadet any longer. Fleetingly he thought of Roger, who didn't stand a chance of reaching Ganymede on a single solo hop from Earth in a ship the size of the *Space Knight*. The *Polaris* unit seemed doomed.

With Kit Barnard in one jet boat, Astro strapped himself into the control chair of the other, and intercoms on, they gently fed power into their ships. Coordinating perfectly in their maneuvers, they headed back to the spaceport with their strange cargo.

Slowly and gently, Kit and Astro circled lower and lower until the two jet boats were directly over the Deimos spaceport. They circled wide and shut off power together, coming down in a long, easy glide. Keeping the cables taut between them, so the chamber wouldn't touch the concrete strip, the two spacemen made perfect landings, coming to a stop directly in front of the control tower. Astro was out of his ship in a flash and almost immediately Kit was beside him. They took no notice of the stereo reporter who was focusing his camera on their efforts to force open the portal on the chamber. Nor did they notice the immense crowd, standing behind police lines, watching and waiting in silence.

"A cutting torch!" bellowed Astro to the emergency crew below. "Get me a cutting torch."

In an instant the torch was handed to him, and ripping the space gloves off his hands, the big cadet began cutting into the tough metal side of the chamber.

The seconds ticked into minutes. The crowds did not move, and only the low comments of the stereo reporter talking over an interplanetary network could be heard above the hiss of the torch as Astro bent to his task. A half hour passed. Astro didn't move or turn away from the blinding light of the torch as he cut into the section of the chamber where the portal locks would be. He did not notice that the *Good Company* and the emergency fleet had returned to the spaceport, nor that Sid was now beside him with Kit.

An hour passed. It seemed to the big cadet that the metal he was cutting, alloyed to protect spacemen against the dangers of the void, was now threatening to cost Tom's life, if indeed he still survived. No one could live long under such conditions unless they had a fresh supply of oxygen. Kit tried to take the torch away from Astro, but the giant Venusian would not let him have it. Again and again, the tanks of fuel supplying the torch were emptied and quickly replaced with fresh ones.

There was something awe-inspiring about the big cadet as he crouched over the torch, its white-hot flame reflected in his grim features. Everyone around him watched in silent fascination, aware that this was a rare exhibition of devotion toward a comrade. They all were certain that Astro would reach Tom—or die in the attempt.

"Touchdown!" Captain Strong called into the ship's intercom. "Secure stations."

The rocket cruiser *Polaris* had just settled on the blast-stained concrete of the Titan spaceport after a blazing flight nonstop from Earth. A Solar Guard cruiser, the most powerful class of spaceship in the Solar Alliance, the *Polaris* was also equipped with hyperdrive, a well-guarded secret method of propulsion, enabling Solar Guard ships to travel through space faster than any other craft known. Many commercial shipping companies, including those entered in the race to Titan, had pleaded for the use of hyperdrive on their ships but were summarily refused. It was one of the strongest weapons in the entire Solar Alliance.

As Commander Walters released the straps holding him securely in his acceleration chair and stepped up beside Strong, the Solar Guard captain gestured toward the teleceiver screen on the bulkhead.

"We're being met by the local officials, sir," he said.

"Ummm," was the commander's laconic reply as he studied the screen. "There's Captain Howard."

"He doesn't look any too happy, sir," commented Strong.

"How would you feel if you had just spent seven years building up the mine operations here on Titan and then have something like this happen to you?"

Strong shook his head. "You're right, sir. I forgot that Howard asked for this duty."

"It's strange how a man will take to a place," mused Walters. "The first time he returned to the Academy, after a tour of duty here on Titan, he looked like a man who had just fallen in love." Walters chuckled. "And in a way I guess he had. He put in for immediate permanent duty here and went back to school to learn all about the mining operations. He, more than anyone else in the Solar Guard, is responsible for our success here."

"Well, are you ready to leave the ship, sir?" asked Strong.

"Yes," replied the commander, but he continued to stare at the teleceiver screen. Strong waited respectfully and finally Walters turned back to him, shaking his head. "The spaceport looks pretty deserted," was his only comment.

Strong had already noticed the desolate appearance of the ordinarily buzzing spaceport and it troubled him more than he would show. He knew that unless the defect in the force fields was corrected soon, the outer-space colony would have to be abandoned to the deadly methane ammonia atmosphere. And to Strong, who had seen the dead satellite before the Solar Guard had discovered crystal there, it was like seeing an old friend sick with a deadly disease. In addition, the hundreds of thousands of colonists would have to be relocated if the force fields could not be repaired and the effect on the economy of the whole Solar

Alliance would be disastrous.

Walters and Strong were met at the airlock by Captain Howard. "I'm awfully glad to see you, sir," he said, coming to attention and saluting smartly. "Hello, Steve. Welcome to Titan."

"Glad to be here, Joe," said Strong.

"We came out as soon as we received your report that you had started evacuation," said Walters. "Have you discovered anything new?"

Howard shook his head. "Not a thing, Commander," he replied. "We've done just about everything but take the force-field projectors apart, but so far we haven't found a thing wrong."

"Any word on the race, Joe?" asked Strong.

Howard looked surprised. "By the stars, I almost forgot. One of the ships is trying to make it to Ganymede without stopping at Deimos for refueling. And another blew up."

Strong gasped. "Which one?"

"*Space Lance*," said Howard. "Exploded over Deimos right after blast-off. *Knight* is the one that's trying the long solo hop. Haven't received any word from him yet."

"But what about the crew of the *Space Lance*?" demanded Strong with a glance at Walters.

"The pilot, Sticoon, was killed, and they haven't found Cadet Corbett yet." And then understanding flashed in Howard's eyes. "Say, that's one of the boys in your unit, isn't it, Steve?" he asked.

"Yes," said Strong grimly. He turned to Walters. "Have I your permission to contact Deimos for the latest details, sir?"

"Of course, Steve. Go ahead."

Strong turned quickly and climbed into a nearby jet boat. The enlisted spaceman at the controls sent the tiny vessel skimming across the broad expanse of the spaceport toward the control tower.

Walters and Howard watched him leave. "I hope nothing has happened to that boy," said Walters. "Corbett is one of the finest cadets we have."

"I'm afraid it doesn't look too good, sir," Howard answered.

"Well, what about the other ship, *Space Knight*?" asked Walters. "Cadet Manning is on that one. Any report on where they are?"

"Nothing, sir," replied Howard. "We just heard that he was bypassing Deimos and going on right through to Ganymede, hoping to get a jump on the other two."

"Did Cadet Manning make that report?" asked Walters.

"No, sir. It was the pilot. Quent Miles. There was no mention of Cadet Manning, sir."

Walters shook his head. "Certainly is strange," he mused aloud. Then he barked, in his usual brusque manner, "Well, we've got this problem here to worry about now. All mining operations have stopped, I suppose?"

"Yes, sir. The men won't work unless they have a guarantee that their wives and children are safe."

"Can't blame them," said Walters, surveying the quiet spaceport.

The two Solar Guard officers climbed into another waiting jet boat and shot away from the *Polaris* toward the tower.

Inside the shimmering crystal control tower, Steve Strong paced up and down behind the enlisted spaceman trying to contact the Deimos spaceport across the millions of miles of space.

"This is Titan spaceport calling Deimos spaceport! Come in, Deimos spaceport."

There was a flood of static, and then, very faintly, the voice of the tower operator on Deimos answered. "This is Deimos spaceport. Go ahead, Titan."

"Transmitting request for information by Captain Steve Strong of the Solar Guard," the Titan operator called into the microphone. "Information concerning explosion of rocket ship *Space Lance*. Please give details on survivors."

There was a momentary pause and the loudspeaker crackled with static. The voice of the Deimos operator broke through. "Captain Sticoon dead. Cadet Corbett believed trapped in airlock chamber. They have just cut through the chamber. It will be a few minutes before I can give you any further information."

"Very well, Deimos. I will hold this channel open."

Walters and Howard entered the room. "Any word,

Strong?" asked the commander. Strong shook his head.

The loudspeaker over the control panel crackled into life again. "Ganymede station to Titan spaceport! Come in, Titan!"

The three Solar Guard officers looked at each other in surprise as the Titan operator acknowledged the call. "This is Titan. Go ahead, Ganymede."

"We have just received word that the rocket ship *Space Knight* is within five minutes of a touchdown this spaceport. Will probably blast off again immediately after refueling. Acknowledge, Titan!"

"I read you, Ganymede!" replied the Titan operator.

"What is your estimated time of arrival at Titan?"

The Ganymede operator was silent a moment, then announced a time that made Strong and Walters blink in amazement. "It is based on his speed from Earth to this point, Titan."

"Very well, Ganymede. End transmission," said the Titan man, closing his key.

Captain Howard stared at Strong and Walters in amazement. "I can't believe it." Strong shook his head. "It's fantastic!"

"I know it is, gentlemen," said a voice in back of them. "But nevertheless, the Ganymede station confirms it."

Strong, Walters, and Howard spun around to look into the smiling face of Charley Brett.

Before anyone could say anything, the voice of the Deimos operator broke the stunned silence. "Deimos to Titan, I have your information now. Are you ready, Titan?"

"Go ahead, Deimos," said the Titan man.

And then, as Strong held his breath, the metallic voice from the loudspeaker reported on the final result of the tragic explosion over Deimos.

10 "...Chamber was cut open and Corbett was rushed to the spaceport's sick bay...."

As the metallic voice of the Deimos tower operator continued his report of the tragic crash of the *Space Lance*, Strong and Walters sighed with relief. At least Tom was not dead!

"He is still in a state of shock, but after a preliminary examination, the medical officer reports that he will recover. That is all the information I have at this time, Titan. End transmission." The loudspeaker was silent except for the continuous flow of static.

"By the stars," breathed Strong, "I'm sure glad to hear that."

Walters put his arm around the captain's shoulder. "I'm glad too, Steve. I know how you feel about those three boys."

"And that Astro," said Strong, beaming. "Wouldn't you know he'd be the one to rescue Tom." He paused and then continued thoughtfully, "You know, sir, with the exception of Manning, I'd be willing to recommend Solar Guard commissions for the unit right now."

Walters snorted. "Manning! By the stars, he could be the best astrogator in the universe, but—but he's so undisciplined."

"Excuse me, sir," the enlisted spaceman interrupted. "Here is a transcript of the report from Deimos if you care to have it."

"Thank you," said Walters, putting it into his pocket. "Well, Steve, I guess we'd better start to work here." He turned to the Titan senior officer who had been waiting respectfully.

"Ready, Captain Howard?"

"Yes, sir."

"Lead on, then," said Walters.

As the three officers turned to leave the control tower, they noticed Charley Brett sitting near the door. In the excitement of the news of Tom's narrow escape, they had forgotten the company owner was there.

Strong stopped and looked at him coldly. "What are you doing on Titan, Brett?"

"Came on ahead to welcome the winner," Brett replied easily, not even bothering to stand.

"Pretty confident your man will win, eh?"

"Most assuredly," said Brett with elaborate sarcasm. "I would never have entered a ship in the race if I didn't think I would win. Though, in all fairness, I think I should have received the contract to haul the crystal without this extra effort."

"What kind of reactant is Quent Miles using in that ship of yours?" asked Walters sharply.

Brett smiled. "The same as everyone else, Commander."

"What about your feeders?" asked Strong. "With ordinary reactant, and no new cooling units aboard your ship, you must have oversized feeders to make such fantastic speeds."

Brett shrugged and held out his hands in a gesture of innocence. "I don't even know myself, Captain Strong," he said blandly. "It's one reason why I have Quent Miles piloting for me. He has a few tricks that apparently are quite effective."

"I hope they are legitimate tricks, Mr. Brett," said Walters. "Let's go, Steve."

The three officers turned away and left Brett sitting there, smiling triumphantly.

"I think we'd better start from the beginning in our inspection of the screens, Captain Howard," said Walters, as the three officers left the control tower and walked across the spaceport. "First of all, I want a twenty-four-hour watch placed on all operational centers, pump houses, and generator plants. I cannot discount the idea of sabotage. Why anyone would want to wreck the screens is beyond me, but we cannot ignore the possibility."

"I already have men stationed at the main operational centers, sir," replied Howard. "Your Space Marines will help me cover the rest."

"Steve," said Walters, turning to the Solar Guard officer, "if this is a natural phenomenon—some new element in Titan's atmosphere breaking down the force screens—the problem is bad enough. But if this is caused by man—if it really is sabotage—we'll have a doubly hard time. We can find the reason eventually, if it is natural, but man can conceal his reasons. And until we find out the motives behind this we must count on the situation getting worse. I want you to pursue *that* line of investigation. Find out if anyone has a good reason to force the abandonment of Titan."

"It's a big order, sir," said Strong. "I'll do the best I can."

"That's good enough for me," replied the commander, nodding his satisfaction.

"ANY WORD, SIR?" ASKED ASTRO EAGERLY as the white-clad medical officer emerged from the room.

The man smiled. "Thanks to you, Cadet Astro," he replied, "your friend will be able to leave as soon as he gets his pants on."

"Yeow!" bawled Astro in his famous bull-like bellow. "Thanks, sir. Thanks a million!" He turned and wrenched open the sick-bay door, almost splintering it in his enthusiasm. Tom was just sitting up on the side of the bed.

"Hiya, Astro!" called Tom with a weak grin. "The sawbones tells me I owe you a brand-new shiny credit piece for saving my life."

His enthusiasm at high pitch, Astro was nevertheless unable to do more than smile broadly at his unit mate. "Only reason I did it," he said.

"All right, here you are." Tom handed over a coin. "That's all I thought my chances were worth."

At that moment the Solar Guard major in command of the Deimos spaceport entered, followed by Kit Barnard and Sid. After greeting Tom with enthusiasm that matched Astro's, Kit and Sid stood to one side quietly and listened while Tom gave his preliminary report to the major who held a recorder microphone in front of him.

"I heard a terrific noise on the power deck as soon as we blasted off," Tom began. "And Captain Sticoon ordered me to go below and check on it. I saw the trouble right away. The lead baffles around the reactant chambers had become loose and the reactant was spilling out, starting to wildcat. I called Bill over the intercom right away and he ordered me to get into a space suit and wait for him in the airlock. I heard him shut off the generators—but that's all. The reactant blew and I must've been knocked cold, because the next thing I remember was this big ugly face bending over me ordering me to wake up." Tom grinned at Astro.

"I see," mused the major aloud. "Now about the baffles. How could they have worked loose? Do you think the lock bolts gave way in the excessive heat due to the intense blast-off speed?"

"No, sir," said Tom firmly. "Those bolts were loosened. I distinctly remember seeing one of them fall to the deck as I walked in."

"Then you suspect that the ship was sabotaged?"

"That's not for me to say, sir," said Tom after a moment's hesitation. "In all my experience, I have never seen one of those bolts work loose of its own accord or because of heat or vibration on the power deck." He glanced at Astro, who was hunched forward, listening intently. "Have you, Astro?"

The big Venusian shook his head slowly. "Never," he said.

"Well, thank you, Corbett, that will be all for now," said the major and then turned to Kit. "I want to congratulate you, sir, on your sacrifice in going to the aid of the *Space Lance*."

"Wild Bill would have done the same thing for me," said Kit without emotion. "Do I have permission to continue the race now?"

The major was startled. "You mean you still want to go on?"

"Every cent I have is tied up in my ship and in this race, sir," said Kit. "I have my new reactor unit working properly now, and I believe that I still have a chance."

"But you've lost hours, man," protested the major.

"I can make them up, sir," said Kit. "Am I permitted to carry on?"

The major was flustered, but nodded his head. "By all means. Yes, indeed! And spaceman's luck to you."

"I'd like to make the trip with him if he'll have me, sir," said Tom, getting off the bed. "I'm all right. The doctor said so."

"But—but—but you need rest, Cadet Corbett," said the major. "No, I can't permit it."

Just at that moment the medical officer walked in.

"So far as I'm concerned," he said, looking at Tom, "he's a lot healthier than you are, sir. With all due respect, sir."

"Very well, then," shrugged the major. "Carry on! Do as you please!" Shaking his head in confusion, the major left the room.

"Well," said Kit Barnard, stepping forward, a big smile on his face, "what are we waiting for?"

"MINUS FIVE, FOUR, THREE, TWO, ONE— *ZERO!*"

The spaceship *Good Company* shot away from the small moon of Mars and thousands of eyes at the spaceport followed it into the heavens, watching its blazing track disappear into the depths of space. If sympathy and good wishes could decide the race to Titan, the spaceship *Good Company* was a certain winner.

Aboard the sleek craft, Tom Corbett relaxed after the tremendous blast-off acceleration and turned to look at the tense face of Kit Barnard who was seated in the pilot's chair.

"Why don't you get some sleep, Kit?" said Tom. "I can take this baby over. It's the least I can do for all you've done for me."

"Thanks, Tom, but I'll stay with it awhile longer," replied the veteran spaceman. "At least until we find out where the *Space Knight* is."

Tom suddenly remembered the trouble with Roger.

"Has there been any news of them at all?" he asked.

"The last thing we heard was that he was approaching Ganymede. And that was a few hours ago, when you were trapped in the air-lock chamber."

"Ganymede!" Tom was thunderstruck. "But—but—how

did he do it?"

Kit shook his head. "I don't know, Tom, but he sure has some speed in that black ship of his."

"Ganymede!" Tom repeated in bewilderment. It was beyond belief. The *Polaris*, using hyperdrive, could scarcely have made the flight any faster. Tom felt his heart sinking. The hope that Kit Barnard could catch the black *Space Knight* was faint now.

"Shall I call Ganymede again and see if they have anything new?" Tom asked finally.

"Yes, do that, Tom," Kit replied.

The curly-haired cadet quickly climbed the ladder to the radar bridge and sat wearily in front of the teleceiver.

"Spaceship *Good Company* to Ganymede spaceport," he called. "Come in, Ganymede."

Seconds later, the voice of the Ganymede control operator crackled over the loud-speaker in reply. "Ganymede station to *Good Company*. Go ahead."

"Can you give me any information on the departure time of *Space Knight* from Ganymede?"

"She has not blasted off yet. She is having trouble in her after burners."

"How long do you estimate it will take for her to effect repairs and blast off?" asked Tom, a note of rising hope in his voice. While the black ship had made it to Ganymede under full power without refueling, the strain might have damaged her seriously. Tom waited patiently for the reply, drumming his fingers on the table in his excitement.

"Not more than sixteen hours, *Good Company*," the Ganymede operator finally answered. "Where are you now?"

Tom quickly ascertained his position and relayed it to the tiny Jovian-moon station. "Space sector fourteen, chart B for baker." After the metallic voice had repeated the information, Tom asked for information on Roger Manning.

"No such person has reported to this office, Cadet Corbett," came the negative reply. "End transmission."

"End transmission," said Tom gloomily and slumped back into his chair. Something had happened to Roger, or he had completely blown his top. And in the light of past performances by the blond-haired radar expert, Tom could not decide which. Roger had threatened many times that if he should ever leave the Academy, he would do it quietly, without fanfare.

There was no better place to drop out of sight than on Ganymede, for it was here that the deep spacers, gigantic spaceships that hauled supplies to the colonies of Alpha Centauri, Tara, and Roald made their last stop. If Roger had finally made good his threat to leave the Academy, Ganymede was the logical place to do it.

But why?

11 "YEOW!"

ASTRO'S BULL-LIKE ROAR ECHOED THROUGH THE *GOOD COMPANY.* Tom and Kit jumped around in their seats to stare dumfounded at the half-stripped cadet climbing through the hatch into the power deck, followed by Sid. Sweating, his body streaked with grease, the belt of rocket-man's tools swinging from his hips, Astro pounded the two spacemen on the back. "We did it!" he roared, turning to hug Sid who was equally grimy and naked to the waist.

"Did what?" demanded Kit.

"You know that bypass feeder you said wouldn't hold a pressure of more than D-18 rate?" said Astro eagerly.

When Kit nodded, Astro roared triumphantly, "Well, it'll hold more than D-18 rate now!"

"What do you mean?" demanded Kit.

Astro's involved and detailed reply in engineering terms

was almost gibberish to Tom, but he understood enough of the unit construction to sense that Astro had done something extraordinary.

"And he did it all himself, too," said Sid quietly. "I didn't do anymore than hold the tools."

"But I still don't understand," protested Kit. "The bypass won't take more than D-18."

"We built another one," said Astro proudly. "Since you were making a small unit, you naturally built a small bypass feeder. We made a big one." Astro grinned. "I admit that it looks a little lopsided, with that tank joint on the side nearly twice as big as the whole cooling unit, but if you'll cut your motors and give me fifteen minutes to change that line, I'll give you a reactant feed at D-30 rate."

"D-D-30," stammered Kit. "You're space happy!" He glanced over at Sid. "Is that right, Sid?" he asked, almost hesitantly.

The youth nodded. "It'll work, Kit. And believe me, I didn't have a thing to do with it. It was his idea and I thought he was nuts too. But he can holler louder than I can and—well, he's bigger'n I am and—" Sid shrugged his shoulders. "He went and did it."

"I want to see that thing for myself!" exclaimed Kit, jumping out of his seat. "Take over for a while, Tom."

Tom slid under the controls of the sleek ship, and while Astro, Sid, and Kit went below to the power deck, he began to figure their speed at a D-30 rate. He used a pencil at first, scribbling on a piece of paper, but the answer he reached was so fabulous, he put the ship on automatic gyro control and climbed to the radar deck where he checked the figures on the electronic calculator. When the result was the same, he let out a whoop.

When he returned to the control deck again, Astro, Kit, and Sid were already working the master control panel, adjusting some of the controls to take the enormous increase in speed. Kit grinned up at Tom. "Here we go, Tom," he said. "This is going to be the fastest ride you've ever had next to hyperdrive."

"Then it really works?" yelled the cadet.

"It not only works, but from the looks of that thing, we'll

use very little more fuel. So now it's our turn to bypass a fuel stop! We're going right on through to Titan!"

"YOU'RE WHISTLING INTO THE WIND, BARNARD!" Quent Miles' voice was harsh and derisive as it crackled over the audioceiver. "You could never catch up with me in a hundred light years! This race is in the bag for yours truly!"

Across the vast distance of space that separated the two speeding ships, Tom, Astro, and Kit Barnard listened to Miles' bragging voice and smiled at each other. All Kit ever wanted was a fair chance, and now, thanks to Astro and Sid, he had better than a fair chance. With their added speed, Tom calculated that the two ships would arrive at the Titan spaceport at about the same time. Only scant minutes separated their estimated times of arrival.

"How much farther do you think that wagon of yours will hold out, Barnard?" continued Miles over the audioceiver. "You'll burn it up or shake it apart. This race is in the bag!"

"All right, Miles," interrupted Tom. "We'll do our talking at the Titan spaceport. Now let me talk to Roger."

"You mean, Manning?" asked Miles, after an almost imperceptible pause.

"Yes, I mean Manning!" snapped Tom.

"Can't oblige, Corbett," said Quent Miles. "Your pal took it on the lam back at Ganymede. He ran out on me. As far as I know, he's still there. Didn't you see him when you stopped for refueling?"

"We didn't stop," said Tom. "What do you mean, he got off at Ganymede? He's supposed to stay with you throughout the race."

"I gotta go now, Corbett," came Miles' abrupt reply. "I'm hittin' rough stuff here, a swarm of meteors. See you on Titan. Be down there to welcome you in."

"Wait! What about Roger?" Tom called frantically into the audioceiver, but Quent Miles did not answer. The young cadet slammed the microphone down on the table. "That blasted Roger!" he cried hotly. "When I get my hands on him, I'm going to—"

"Take it easy, Tom," said Astro, putting a hand on the cadet's shoulder. "You know how Roger is. Wait until he has a chance to explain before you blast him."

"I suppose you're right, Astro," replied Tom. "But why in the stars would he leave the ship?"

"Whatever he's done, I'm sure Roger has a good explanation," replied the big Venusian. But inwardly he couldn't help feeling that Roger, somehow, had gotten into another scrape which would, in the end, reflect on the whole unit. Neither Tom nor Astro cared much for their own individual reputations, but they were concerned about the record of the unit. Roger had managed to pull himself out of some narrow scrapes, but there was always the first time for everything. Leaving his post as monitor in the race was as serious as anything he had done so far.

"Heads up, Tom!" Kit called out. "Meteor storm in our course. We've got to change our heading."

"Aye, aye, sir," replied the young cadet, pushing aside his concern over his unit mate and concentrating on routine flight operations.

On and on, the sleek ship plummeted through the black depths of space beyond Jupiter, heading for the planet Saturn and her magnificent rings of different colors, and to her largest satellite with its deadly methane ammonia gas atmosphere, the crystal-bearing moon, Titan.

"THEY ARE APPROACHING THE SPACEPORT, SIR," called the Titan control-tower operator, and Strong jumped to the radarscope to stare at the two blips on the screen. Only a mile separated them, with Quent Miles' *Space Knight* ahead.

"Five minutes to touchdown," reported the operator.

"Come on, Kit," muttered Strong through clenched teeth. "Pour it on, boy. Give her the gun!"

The two blips drew closer to the heart of the scope. First one and then the other shooting ahead for brief seconds as they began deceleration.

"You can see them outside, now, sir," said the operator, and Strong jumped to the door, stepping out on the observation platform that looked out over the spaceport. He searched the skies above him, and then, faintly, he could see the exhaust trails of the two ships as they streaked over the field, beginning their deceleration orbits around the satellite.

Behind him, Strong heard the voice of the tower operator ordering Ramp Four and Ramp Five cleared for the two ships, and the mobs of people on the spaceport surged back. Strong noted the irony of the situation. The people of Titan were not out to greet a hero of space, but were waiting for the next evacuation rocket ship.

The ramps were cleared and within minutes the two ships reappeared over the horizon, nosing upward over the spaceport in an arc, their braking rockets blasting loudly as they prepared to land.

Then, feeling that his heart would stop, Captain Strong saw Quent Miles' black ship touch the surface of the spaceport first. Kit Barnard had lost the race. By seconds to be sure, but he had lost the race.

A weak cheer arose from the crowds and then quickly died out. To them the race was futile and the prize empty. How could the winning company ship crystal when, soon, none would be mined?

Strong raced across the field and boarded the *Good Company* to find Kit, Tom, Astro, and Sid sitting glumly on the control deck. There was a quick smile of greeting on the two cadets' faces when they saw their unit commander, but their smiles died away. Abruptly Kit Barnard was on his feet looking past Strong to someone entering the hatch behind him.

"Congratulations, Quent!" said Kit, extending his hand. "That was a great race."

"Thanks," replied Miles. "But I never figured it would end any other way. You put up a great fight, Barnard. Yes, sir! A great fight!" He turned to Captain Strong and chortled. "Good race, eh, Strong?"

The Solar Guard officer shook hands with the winner and then asked, "Where is Cadet Manning?"

"Say, I want to make a complaint about that!" exclaimed Miles. He looked at Tom and Astro. "It was bad enough to have to be bothered with these kids, but when they behave the way that kid Manning behaved, I've got a right to be sore!"

"When did Manning leave the ship?" asked Strong.

"As soon as we made touchdown on Ganymede. He left

the ship after sleeping all the way out, made a couple of nasty cracks, and the last I saw of him, he was heading over toward the deep-space section of the spaceport."

"You're sure of that?" asked Strong.

Quent Miles sneered. "I just said that's what happened, didn't I?"

"Yes, that's what you said," Strong replied. "And I'll have to take your word for it until Manning can answer for himself."

"How did you manage to make it from Earth to Ganymede without refueling, Quent?" asked Kit slowly. "And what have you got in your ship to get that kind of speed?"

Miles' lips curled in a twisted grin. "That's my secret, spaceman," he said, turning away. "Well, I've got to report to my boss. Great race, Kit. Too bad there couldn't be more than one winner." He laughed and swaggered out of the ship.

"I'd like to brain that guy," growled Tom.

"All right, Corbett, Astro, pack your gear and report to the control tower for reassignment," snapped Strong. He turned and with a nod of sympathy to Kit left the control deck.

"Let's go, Astro," sighed Tom. "We'll see you later, Kit. You too, Sid. And—" They looked at each other, but there was nothing more that could be said. The race was finished.

When Tom and Astro had finished packing their gear and left the ship, Sid turned to Kit. "I'm going to take a look at the *Space Knight*!" he announced.

"Better not, Sid." Barnard shook his head. "Miles is a rough customer. He might not like visitors around his 'secret' on the power deck."

Sid's face was set. "I'm going," he repeated and ducked through the hatch.

His face showing his disappointment at having lost the race, Kit paced the deck for a moment and then he strode purposefully toward the hatch, calling:

"Hey! Wait, Sid. I'm coming with you."

In the control tower at the far end of the spaceport, Tom and Astro entered the station commander's office in time to overhear the last of Commander Walters' orders to Captain Strong.

"...Might as well give the boys a rest before we begin our investigations, Steve." He looked up as the door opened. "Oh, here they are now."

"Cadets Corbett and Astro reporting, sir." Tom and Astro saluted smartly.

"Stand easy, boys," said Walters, rising to face them. "I don't know how much you've heard of this emergency on Titan, but you can be briefed on details later. For the moment, all you have to know is that your assignment here is concerned with a detailed checking-out of the whole force-screen machinery. Take a twenty-four-hour rest and then report back here ready for the hardest work you'll ever do in your lives."

"Yes, sir," said Tom.

"Where is Manning? Didn't he think it necessary to report to me?" Walters looked at Strong. "Well, Steve? It's your unit?"

"It seems he got off the *Space Knight* at Ganymede, sir," replied Strong reluctantly. "Captain Miles said the last he saw of Manning he was walking toward the deep-space section of the spaceport."

Walters' eyes suddenly became very bright and hard. "He got off, did he? Well," he snapped, "this is just about the end of the line for Cadet Roger Manning!"

"I'm sure Roger has a good explanation, sir—" began Tom.

Walters glared at the cadet. "None of that, Corbett. Manning is a bad rocket and the sooner I get rid of him the better off the Academy and the *Polaris* unit will be. Now take your twenty-four-hours' leave and report back here ready to work."

"Yes, sir," replied Tom. He and Astro saluted and turned to leave the office but were stopped by the sudden appearance of Sid and Kit. Sid's face was aglow. Kit was scowling.

"You know what we found on the *Space Knight*?" exclaimed Sid, unable to hold back.

"What?" asked Tom.

"Almost a full tank of reactant!" replied the young

engineer. "And the after burners showed about as much wear as if the ship had jumped from Earth to Venus."

"What's that, young man?" snapped Walters, stepping forward quickly. "What are you talking about?"

Kit Barnard faced the commander and began to explain.

"We were both curious about Quent Miles' ship, sir," he said. "We wondered what kind of equipment he had to get that kind of speed, so we went aboard and looked her over. She looks as if she just made a routine flight. Hardly any of her baffling has been eaten away and her motors are cooling fast, and I'd swear by the stars there isn't anything on that ship to give her the kind of speed she made out here."

"Hm-m! There's something funny about this," mused Walters.

Strong stepped forward quickly. "Would you like me to investigate, sir?" he asked eagerly.

"Of course not," snapped Walters. "What's the matter with you? We've got a whole planet full of people about to lose their homes and you want to take time off to investigate pure speculation!"

"I'm sorry, sir." Strong's face flushed at the rebuke.

"Carry on! Work with Joe Howard."

"Yes, sir."

Strong saluted and started for the door. He passed Tom, Astro, Sid, and Kit without so much as a glance. His jaw was set like a rock.

Tom Corbett shuffled uncomfortably, embarrassed at the rebuke Strong had just suffered from Walters. It was not like the commander to flare up so quickly. The situation on Titan must be extremely serious. He and Astro ducked out of the room quickly.

"Come on, Astro," muttered the young cadet. "Let's get a bite to eat. I'm starved."

"I was," said the giant Venusian. "But I lost my appetite."

"Boy, do I wish I had Roger here now!"

"Yeah, me too!"

12 "OLYMPIA, THE LARGEST COLONY ON TITAN, WAS GRIPPED BY A WAVE OF FEAR. The broad streets were empty; the shops and stores were deserted; and the population waited in line at the spaceport, with their most valuable belongings, for their turn to leave the threatened settlement. Slowly the satellite of Saturn was dying, and through the methane ammonia atmosphere, the glittering rings of the mother planet shone down on her death struggle.

Tom Corbett and Astro walked through the streets, overcome by the desolation around them. Many parts of the city were completely abandoned, and the few remaining citizens wore cumbersome oxygen masks as the deadly atmosphere of gas seeped through the force field to reach the ground surface of the satellite.

As the two cadets continued their dismal tour, they could only find one small restaurant open, a self-service food center that required no help. They were the only customers. During the meal they hardly talked, as they watched the slow procession of people outside, heading for the spaceport.

When the two cadets left the restaurant, a jet car suddenly blasted to a stop beside them and a master sergeant, dressed in the scarlet red of the enlisted Solar Guard, jumped out to face them.

"All persons are required to wear oxygen masks, Cadets," the sergeant announced, handing over two masks. "And I would suggest that you leave this section of the city as quickly as possible. The screens are leaking badly again. We may have to close off this section too."

Tom and Astro took the masks but did not put them on.

"Thanks, Sergeant," said Tom. "But we'll probably be around here for some time. We're on special duty with Commander Walters and Captain Strong."

At the mention of Strong's name, the sergeant started, looked at the boys closely, and then smiled. "Say, aren't you Corbett and Astro?"

"That's right," acknowledged Tom.

"Well, don't you remember me?" asked the sergeant.

Tom looked at him closely and then smiled in sudden recognition. "Morgan! Phil Morgan!" he cried.

"Of course," chimed in Astro.

"Sure," said the sergeant. "We went through our first test together at the Academy and I washed out."

"And you became an enlisted man!" exclaimed Tom. "Man, you're a real space buster!"

"I figured if I couldn't get into space one way, I'd do it another," said Morgan proudly. "A lot of times I wished I was still a cadet with you, but now I don't think I'd change it for anything in the world."

"I can believe that," said Tom, smiling. "And a master sergeant at that! McKenny told us once it took a man nearly fifteen years to get top rating. It must really be a labor of love for you to have made it this quickly." He stuck out his hand. "Congratulations, Morgan."

They shook hands. "Well, I've got to get rolling," said Morgan. "I sure hope you fellows find out what's cooking here. I've got a lot of friends here and they stand to lose everything they own if Titan is abandoned."

"With Captain Strong on the job, you can bet we'll find out the trouble," declared Astro.

Morgan smiled. "See you around," he said, and jumped back into the jet car. A second later it was roaring down the street to the western part of the city.

"Boy, sure makes you feel good to know that a guy loves

space so much that he would fight his way to the top of the enlisted guard as Morgan did!" said Tom.

Suddenly Astro jerked Tom by the sleeve and pulled him back into the restaurant to crouch behind the door.

"Hey, what's the matter with you?" growled Tom.

"Sh-h-h!" hissed Astro and pointed across the street. "Look!"

Tom poked his head around the corner of the doorway and quickly jerked it back again. Quent Miles was hurrying down the street.

"Wonder what he's doing around here?" whispered Astro, watching the black-clad spaceman pass directly opposite them and continue down the street, seemingly unaware that he was being watched.

"He must be heading for the evacuated section," said Tom.

"How do you figure that?" asked Astro, as they peered cautiously around the edge of the doorway.

"He's wearing his oxygen mask."

"Come on!" said Astro. "Let's find out what that heel is up to."

Hugging the buildings, the two cadets walked down the street, following Miles. There was a puzzled frown on Astro's face as he stared at the spaceman, a hundred feet away. "I swear, Tom," he complained, "I'm about to bust a rocket. Every time I see that guy, I think I know him, but when I try to pin it down, it slips away from me."

"Watch it!" cried Tom. "He's stopping."

The boys ducked behind a deserted jet car as Quent Miles suddenly spun around to stare suspiciously back down the street.

"I don't know if he saw us or not," whispered Tom.

"With that oxygen mask," replied the big cadet, "maybe he can't see very well."

"He's going on," replied Tom. "Come on. We've got to find out what he's up to. He wouldn't be concerned about someone following him if he weren't trying to hide something."

They slipped around the jet car and stepped back on the sidewalk. Ahead of them, Quent Miles was walking quickly, reading all the street signs. Suddenly he turned down a side street, and the two cadets raced after him.

They were in the outskirts of the city now. Great areas were covered with rolling grass fields where the citizens of Titan spent their leisure hours playing ball and picnicking, and it was easy for the cadets to follow the black-suited spaceman. They had to put on their oxygen masks as the deadly fumes of the methane ammonia atmosphere began to swirl around them. They were near the outer limits of the atmosphere screen's effectiveness.

"I think he's going into that building up ahead, Astro," said Tom, his voice distorted to a low metallic hiss by the miniature amplifier in the face of the mask.

Astro nodded and they ducked into a gully as Quent Miles turned once again and glanced down the street.

"Wonder what's in that building?" mused Tom.

"One way to find out," said Astro. "Come on. He's moving again."

The gas began to thicken now, and the two cadets found it difficult to see more than a few feet ahead as they moved cautiously through the swirling death around them. After what seemed like an hour, but was actually hardly more than a few minutes, they found the building Miles had entered.

"I'd give two weeks' leave for a ray gun now," said Tom.

"Want me to try the door?" asked Astro.

"Go ahead. We can't learn anything standing out here."

Astro put his hand on the circular latch and twisted it slowly. The door slid back on rollers, exposing a dark interior. The two boys slipped inside.

"Better close the door, Astro," said Tom. "The ammonia doesn't seem to be so thick in here."

Astro twisted the latch on the inner side and the heavy door rolled back into place. They turned slowly and saw a room that was dark except for a single light gleaming weakly through the haze of the gas. When their eyes became adjusted to the semidarkness, they moved, searching for another door in the huge room.

"Are you sure this is the right place?" asked Astro.

"I can't be positive," said Tom. "The stuff outside was too thick—" He stopped, touched Astro on the arm, and pointed to his left. There was the sound of a door sliding back and light filtered into the murky room. Quent Miles stood framed in the doorway, the unmistakable outline of a paralo-ray gun in his right hand.

"Drop to the floor," hissed Tom.

The two cadets dropped lightly to the floor and lay face down, while Quent Miles walked toward them fanning the gun around menacingly. Then, as he was about to step on Astro's hand, he turned and walked quickly back to the door. "You must be nuts, Charley," the two cadets heard him say. "There's nobody here."

The door rolled closed and the light was cut off. Tom and Astro rose and quietly made their way toward the door. They stopped, leaned against the door, and tried to hear what was going on inside, but were unable to distinguish more than a vague mumble of voices, because of their masks and the thickness of the door. Suddenly, however, they were conscious of footsteps approaching from the other side.

There was no time to hide. Each boy flattened himself against the wall on opposite sides of the door and held his breath as the door opened slowly.

"There can be no doubt about it, Steve," said Commander Walters to the young captain. "What we need are more powerful pumping stations for oxygen *and* additional generators for supplying power to the force field."

"How do you figure that, sir?" asked Strong.

"It's simply this," replied Walters. "The population here has nearly tripled in the past two years. The force-field screens were set up originally to accommodate only a minimum number of miners and their families. With the heavy demand for crystal, and therefore, more civilians to dig it out, the force field has been overloaded."

"But I still don't see how, sir," Strong protested.

"The more people, the more oxygen needed to keep them alive, right?"

Strong nodded.

"The force screens hold back the methane ammonia gas and create a vacuum into which we pump oxygen, right?"

Again Strong nodded.

"Now we have a demand for more and more oxygen, and

we pump it into the vacuum, but eventually we arrive at the point where the pressure of the oxygen inside is greater than the pressure outside. Therefore, the screening force field is broken in its weaker points and the oxygen escapes. When the balance is restored, the rupture isn't sealed and gas seeps in."

Strong glanced questioningly at Captain Howard and at Kit Barnard, who had been asked to remain on Titan and lend his assistance to the problem of the screens.

"Well, gentlemen?" asked Walters, noticing Strong's glance. "That is my theory. Do any of you have a better one? Or a more reasonable explanation?"

Strong, Barnard, and Howard shook their heads. A complete check of every possible source of trouble had been made by the four men and they had found nothing.

"We still have to wait for a report from the electronics sections, sir," said Howard, rubbing his eyes. He started to get up and then suddenly slumped to the floor.

"By the craters of Luna!" cried Walters, jumping to the young officer's side. Howard was picked up and placed on a nearby couch. While Strong and Kit loosened his clothing, Walters grabbed the nearest oxygen mask and slipped it over the spaceman's face.

"Funny that he should pass out like that," commented Strong, sniffing the air. "I still don't smell anything."

Kit looked up at Strong and grinned. "He's not gassed. He's asleep."

"Asleep!" exclaimed Walters.

The enlisted spaceman standing on guard at the door stepped forward and saluted smartly. "Captain Howard hasn't slept for the last five days," he said. "He's been working night and day."

Walters smiled. "All right, Sergeant, take him to his quarters." Then he held up his hand. "No, let him stay where he is." He turned to Steve. "Come on, Steve. You too, Kit. Let's see if we can't get a report from the electronics section before we speculate any further."

The three men left the control-tower office under the watchful eyes of a squad of Space Marines. Trouble had already started at the spaceport when a crowd of excited miners had charged a detachment of enlisted men guarding Solar Guard cruisers. The crowds were growing panicky as the deadly gas filled the city, unchecked.

Strong, Walters, and Kit Barnard climbed into a waiting jet car, amid the hoots and catcalls from the waiting miners, and hurtled away to the giant building housing the electronic "brain" that controlled the force-field screens.

Walters' face was grim. Beside him, Strong and Kit were silent as they raced through the empty streets. If there was no positive discovery by the electronics section of the huge screening operations, then it would have to be assumed that Commander Walters was right in his theory of overpopulation. To remedy that situation would require complete reconstruction of the satellite settlement and temporary abandonment of Titan. Millions of dollars would be lost and thousands of people thrown out of work. It would be a severe blow to the Solar Alliance.

The jet car slowed to a stop. They were in front of the electronics building and the three men climbed out wearily. They would know in a few minutes now.

13 **"YOU'RE AFRAID OF YOUR OWN SHADOW!"** Miles snarled over his shoulder to Charley Brett who followed him out of the room. Brett was adjusting his oxygen mask with one hand and gripping a paralo-ray gun tightly with the other.

"Never mind the cracks," snapped Brett, his voice muffled by the mask. "I tell you I heard someone moving around in here."

Miles laughed again and walked straight to the middle of the room. With their backs pressed to the wall beside the door, Tom and Astro saw Miles bend over and lift a trapdoor in the middle of the floor.

The two men flashed a light down into the opening and climbed down, pulling the trapdoor closed after them.

No sooner was it shut than Tom and Astro jumped forward to examine it cautiously. Astro started to pull it open but Tom held out a warning hand. He turned and pointed toward the room that Miles and Brett had left. Astro nodded and they walked quickly back to the door. Sliding it open, they stepped inside.

"By the rings of Saturn!" cried Astro.

"Well, blast my jets!" Tom exclaimed.

The air in the room was clear, completely free of the misty whirling methane ammonia of death that swirled around them outside. Recovering from his surprise quickly, Astro closed the door and walked to the center of the room, looking around curiously. Tom had already slipped off his mask and was examining the equipment lying on the floor. Astro bent over an oddly shaped machine that looked somewhat like an ancient compressed-air drill, with a long bar protruding from one end. He examined the bar closely and then turned slowly to Tom.

"Do you know what this machine is?" he asked in almost a whisper.

Tom looked at it and then shook his head.

"I haven't seen one of these since I left Venus, and then only when I was a kid hanging around the spaceports where the space rats used to blast off for the asteroids looking for uranium."

"You mean you hunt uranium with that thing?" asked Tom.

"No, you dig it out with this."

Tom gazed at the machine thoughtfully. "Why would it be here?" he mused.

"It's already been used," said Astro, standing up. "Look, the drill head is dull."

"That trapdoor!" Tom exclaimed. "It leads to a mine. Miles and Brett have discovered high-grade uranium right here on Titan where everyone thought there was nothing but *crystal!*"

Astro nodded grimly. "And that isn't all. This room is free of ammonia gas."

"But how in the star-blazing dickens can they keep it out of here when everything else outside is flooded with it?" asked Tom.

Astro spun around and began to examine the walls. "Just as I thought!" he exclaimed. "This room is airtight! Sealed! Oxygen is being pumped in here."

"From where?"

"Might be from somewhere below," replied the big Venusian. "Down that trap where Miles and Brett went."

Tom put his mask back on and headed for the door. Astro followed him. They opened it a little and peered into the swirling mist.

"Then it's being pumped in directly," Tom asserted. "Through a duct leading directly up into this room from somewhere below."

Astro nodded. "Then there's only one thing left to do. Go down through that trapdoor and see what we can find." He stepped forward.

"Wait a minute, Astro," said Tom, stopping him. "Let me check our oxygen. There might not be any down there. Remember, Miles and Brett wore *their* masks."

Making a quick check of their oxygen supply, Tom patted Astro on the back and started forward. "It's OK. We've got another four hours left. Come on!"

They moved toward the trapdoor slowly.

"I still wish I had a ray gun," whispered Tom.

"As long as I can use these"—Astro balled his hamlike hands into fists—"we're OK."

When they reached the trapdoor, Tom got down on his knees and felt around for the opening. He found a small ring bolt, motioned to Astro to step back, and pulled. The trapdoor swung back easily and a shaft of white light gleamed in his face. The young cadet leaned down and looked through the opening. What he saw made him gasp.

"What is it?" demanded Astro.

Tom motioned for him to get down and look. The big cadet dropped lightly to his knees to peer through the opening. "By the moons of Jupiter," he exclaimed, "it's a—a mining shaft!"

"Just what we thought it was," whispered Tom. "Come on. Let's go down and find out where it leads."

"Maybe we'd better go back and tell Captain Strong about this first," Astro said speculatively.

"There's no telling what Brett and Miles are liable to do while we're gone," said Tom. "You find Captain Strong and I'll go down into the shaft and look around."

"Not on your life," protested Astro. "You don't think I'd let you go down there alone, do you? *You* go back to Captain Strong and *I'll* see what those two are doing down there."

Tom grinned. "OK, we'll both go down," he said.

Opening the trapdoor all the way, Tom eased himself down into the opening. Astro followed. Immediately below the trap, they found a ladder, fixed to the wall of the shaft, which led directly down to a point about thirty feet below the surface of Titan. At the bottom the two cadets paused. A long tunnel stretched before them.

"Listen to that!" exclaimed Astro.

Tom ripped off the mask and listened. He heard a strange noise which sounded more like the roar of escaping gas than a motor.

"What is it?" asked Tom.

"That's what I'd like to know!"

"And that light," continued Tom, pointing down the length of the tunnel. "Do you suppose it's Miles and Brett?"

"It isn't moving," commented Astro.

"Well, since we're here we might as well find out as much as we can," Tom decided. "Let's go."

The two cadets flattened themselves against the side of the shaft and inched forward. The hissing noise was slowly building up to a roar now, and as they made their way along the shaft, they passed other smaller tunnels that branched off to the left and right. There was evidence of recent work.

Tools were scattered along the tunnel floors, as if the workers had dropped them in sudden flight.

The light ahead of them grew brighter, and as they rounded a corner, they saw a bare, unshaded lamp suspended from the roof of the tunnel.

Tom suddenly stopped and jerked Astro back. "Look!" he exclaimed, pointing to the floor, not two paces away. A thin wire, hardly noticeable, was stretched across the floor at ankle height.

"That bright light is to attract your attention while you trip over that thing and probably blow yourself to bits," he said grimly, pointing to the wall where the wire was connected to a small charge of explosives. "Nothing to bring the roof down," he continued, "but enough to blast whoever tripped over this wire."

Stepping over the wire carefully, they started down the shaft again, but Tom paused thoughtfully.

"What's the matter?" asked Astro.

"That booby trap," said Tom. "We'd better not take any chances of tripping over it on the way back. We might be in a hurry."

"I know what you mean," grunted the big Venusian. He knelt down beside the menacing box of explosives and quickly disconnected the trip wire, throwing the box to one side.

Straightening up, Astro announced, "It's harmless now."

Cautiously the two cadets continued down the tunnel, the roaring sound growing louder and louder. After twenty minutes, Astro paused, his homely features wrinkled in a frown of worry.

"Think maybe Miles and Brett went off into one of the other side tunnels?" he asked.

Tom thought a moment. "No, I don't, Astro. We haven't hit another side tunnel since we passed that booby trap back there. What would be the use of setting that thing up if they went in another direction?"

"There must be another way out of here, then," Astro remarked.

"Why?"

"That part of the tunnel back there by the bomb was

loose dirt. If the bomb had exploded, the whole tunnel would have been blocked off and how could they get out?"

Tom didn't answer. He was thinking about what he was going to do if there should be another booby trap in the tunnel. It was so dark now that they could hardly see more than a few feet ahead. The bright light was merely a pinpoint in the distance behind them.

And then Tom became aware that the roar that had been with them constantly since they had entered the shaft had now lessened in volume. But they had not passed a single branch-off tunnel where the sound could have originated. Tom made up his mind quickly.

"Come on, Astro," he said. "We're going back."

"Why?"

"I haven't time to explain now, but you walk close to one side of the shaft and I'll take the other. Feel along with your hands for anything like a door or an opening. I think we've passed them."

Without another word, Astro turned around and headed back, feeling along the tunnel wall.

It did not take the two cadets long to discover what they were looking for. A heavy wooden door was set flush with the side of the tunnel. And when Tom pressed his ear to it, he could hear the roaring sound throbbing heavily inside.

"See if you can open it, Astro," said Tom. "But take it easy."

Astro felt along the side of the door until he found a wooden latch and he lifted it gently. The door swung back, as if pushed, as a powerful draft caught it from the other side. The roar was now deafening.

Tom stepped inside cautiously, followed by Astro. They found themselves on a small balcony overlooking a huge subterranean room. In the room they saw Quent Miles and Charles Brett bending over a table on which were several delicate electronic instruments. Tom and Astro recognized them immediately as testing machinery for radioactivity, much more advanced and sensitive than the ordinary Geiger counter. Around the two men was ample evidence of Astro's original assumption that they were digging into a hot vein of uranium pitchblende. To one side of the room, lead sheets lined a rough boxlike structure that Astro and Tom guessed was covering for the radioactive vein. Against the wall lay the lead-lined suits used by the miners. Further to one side, Tom saw a huge open pipe. He nudged Astro.

"Look, over there," Tom whispered. "That's where the oxygen is coming from!"

Below them, Miles suddenly walked to the pipe and pulled a large lever on its side. The roaring sound stopped immediately and the boys felt the air pressure in the room lessen slightly.

"That blasted noise is driving me crazy," explained Miles, walking back to the table, his voice echoing in the rock-walled cavern.

Brett, leaning over the table, was stabbing around futilely in one of the sets of tubes in a complicated testing device. "Wish we had that squirt Manning here," he mumbled. "He could fix these things up in no time at all."

"I could always go back to the hideout and get him," suggested Miles.

On the balcony Tom gripped Astro's arm tightly.

"Astro! Did you hear that?" he exclaimed.

The big cadet nodded and started to rise from their place of concealment. Tom pulled him down. "Wait," he whispered sharply. "No use barging in on them yet. Maybe we can find out where Roger is first."

Astro reluctantly crouched down again, his hamlike hands balled into fists.

The two cadets watched Quent Miles and Brett work on the instruments awhile longer. Finally Miles slammed down a pair of wire cutters on the table and growled at Brett. "No use messing with this thing any longer. I don't know what makes it tick, so I can't find the trouble. We need new equipment."

"It'll take at least two weeks to get new equipment the way things are going here at Titan," replied Brett.

"Well, there's no use hanging around here if we can't dig any more of the stuff out, and I ain't going behind that lead shield unless I got a machine that tells me it's safe."

"I've been thinking about Manning," said Brett.

"What about him?"

"Suppose we move the stuff we've already mined to the hideout, and take this equipment along too. He can repair it out there. We can turn off the oxygen that we're sucking off from the Solar Guard pumps, and by the time we get back here, the old satellite will be back to normal. Then, with the equipment repaired and Olympia back to normal, we can really begin operations."

Quent nodded quickly. "Good idea. Come on. Let's get this stuff aboard the ship."

On the balcony Tom and Astro looked at each other.

"They're responsible for what's happened here on Titan!" whispered Tom. "They have been sucking off oxygen from the main pumps supporting the force field."

"Come on, Tom," growled Astro. "My fist is just itching to make contact with a couple of no-good chins."

"Not so fast! We still don't know where they've got Roger."

"You want to keep on following them?" asked Astro.

"At least to their ship," Tom replied. "Then we can notify Captain Strong and he can track them in the *Polaris*. If we barge in on them now, we'll just get the satisfaction of knocking their heads together with no guarantee of any information." The young cadet turned to the door. "We'll sneak up the tunnel a way and then follow them out."

"Hurry!" said Astro. "Here they come." Quent, carrying one of the instruments, had started up the steps to the balcony.

Tom grabbed the latch and pushed up but the door would not open. "Give me a hand, Astro, quick!" he called.

Astro grabbed the latch and heaved his bulk against the door. Suddenly he stepped back dumfounded, holding the latch in his hand. It had snapped off.

Just at that moment Brett looked up and saw them. He shouted a warning to Miles, who dropped the instrument he was carrying and pulled out his ray gun.

"Just stand where you are!" he snarled, leveling the gun at them.

Tom and Astro stood quietly, hands in the air.

"How in blazes did they get here?" Brett cried.

"They must have followed me," said Miles. "They certainly couldn't have known about this place."

"But how did they get past the trap?" Brett persisted, still amazed and shaken by the unexpected appearance of the cadets.

Astro snorted his contempt. "You must think we're a couple of prize space jerks," he growled. "You can't even kill a mouse with that thing now."

"Let's cut the talk," said Miles. "What do we do with them?"

"Freeze them!" snapped Brett. "No telling how long they've been here and how much they know."

"We know enough to put you on a prison asteroid," challenged Tom.

"Freeze 'em, it is," said Quent. "We'll get the ship loaded and decide what to do with them later."

He pressed the trigger on his ray gun. There was a harsh crackling sound and Tom and Astro stiffened into immobility, every nerve and muscle deadened. With the exception of their hearts, and sense of seeing and hearing, they might have been dead men.

Laughing to themselves, Quent Miles and Charles Brett picked up their instruments, walked past them, and disappeared through the door.

14 "CHARLES BRETT SWAGGERED INTO THE CONTROL ROOM OF THE ELECTRONICS BUILDING. Commander Walters, Captain Strong, and Kit Barnard looked up from their study of the reports the chief engineer had handed them.

"What are you doing here, Brett?" demanded Walters. "I thought you had blasted out of here long ago."

"I'm leaving as soon as we sign the contracts for hauling the crystal, Commander," said Brett.

"Contracts!" exploded Strong. "Why, man, do you realize

that this satellite is about to die? If we don't find out what's wrong with the screens, there won't be any crystal mined here for the next ten years."

Brett shook his head and smiled. "That's all right with me too," he said. "The contracts call for either party to satisfy the other should either party fail to fulfill the contractual agreements. In other words, Strong, I get paid for making the trip out to Titan, whether you have crystal to haul or not."

"Why, you dirty—" snarled Strong.

"Just a moment, Steve," Walters interrupted sharply. "Brett's right. We had no way of knowing that this situation would arise, or grow worse than it was in the beginning. Brett went to a great deal of expense to enter the race and win it. If he insists that the Solar Guard abide by the contract, there's nothing we can do but pay."

"It won't be too bad, Commander Walters," said Brett. "I have my ship loaded with crystal now, and if you'll just sign the contracts, I can deliver one cargo of crystal to Atom City before Titan is abandoned."

"Wait a minute," cried Strong. "Who gave you the right to load crystal before signing the contract?"

"I assumed the right, Captain Strong," replied Brett smoothly. "My ship won the race, didn't it? Why shouldn't I start work right away?"

"Well, that's beside the point now, anyway," Walters said. "We may need your ship to take miners and their families to Ganymede or Mars, Brett. Never mind the crystal. One load won't mean very much, anyway."

"No, thank you," growled Brett. "I don't haul any miners in my ship. The contracts call for crystal and that's all."

"I'm ordering you to take those people, Brett," said Walters coldly. "This is an emergency."

"Order all you want," snapped Brett. "Look at your space code book, section four, paragraph six. My rights are fully protected from high-handed orders issued by men like you who think they're bigger than the rest of the people."

Walters flushed angrily. "Get out!" he roared.

"Not till you sign that contract," Brett persisted. "And if I don't leave with a signed contract in my pocket, I'll have you up before the Solar Alliance Council on charges of fraud. You haven't got a leg to stand on and you know it. Now sign that contract."

Abruptly, Walters turned to an enlisted spaceman and instructed him to get his brief case from the *Polaris*, then deliberately turning his back on Brett, continued his study of the report. Strong and Kit Barnard watched Brett with narrowed eyes as the arrogant company owner crossed to the other side of the room and sat down.

"You know something, Steve," said Kit quietly. "Back at the Academy, I failed to register a protest about someone dumping impure reactant into my feeders."

"What about it?" asked Strong.

"I'd like to register that protest now."

"Now?" Steve looked at him, a frown on his face. "Why now?"

"For one thing, Brett couldn't blast off until there was an investigation."

"You might have something there, Kit," replied Strong with a smile. "And since Brett won the race under such— *er*—mysterious circumstances, I'd suggest an investigation of the black ship as well, eh?"

Kit grinned. "Shall I make that a formal request?"

"Right now, if you like."

Kit turned to face Commander Walters. "Commander," he announced, "I would like to register a formal protest with regard to the race."

Walters glanced up. "Race?" he growled. "What the devil are you talking about, Kit?"

"Captain Barnard seems to think that Mr. Brett's ship might have used equipment that was not standard, sir," Strong explained. "In addition, his own ship was sabotaged during the time trials."

Walters looked at Strong and then at Kit Barnard, unable to understand. "What's happened to you two? Bringing up a thing like that at this time. Have you lost your senses?"

"No, sir," replied Kit. "But I believe that if a formal investigation was started, the Solar Guard would be within its legal rights to delay signing the contracts until such investigation was completed."

Walters grinned broadly. "Of course! Of course!"

Brett jumped up and stormed across the room. "You can't get away with this, Walters!" he shouted. "I won this race fairly and squarely. You have to sign that contract."

"Mr. Brett," said Walters coldly, "under the circumstances, I don't have to do a space-blasted thing." He turned to Kit. "Is this a formal request for an investigation, Kit?" He was smiling.

"It is, sir."

"Very well," said Walters, turning to Brett. "Mr. Brett, in the presence of two witnesses, I refuse to sign the contracts as a result of serious charges brought against you by one of the participating entrants. You will be notified of the time and place of the hearing on these charges."

Brett's face turned livid. "You can't do this to me!"

Walters turned to one of the enlisted guardsmen. "Escort Mr. Brett from the room," he ordered.

A tall, husky spaceman unlimbered his paralo-ray rifle and nudged Brett from the room. "I'll get even with you, Walters, if it's the last thing I do," he screamed.

"You make another threat like that to a Solar Guard officer," growled the enlisted spaceman, "and it'll be the *last* thing you do."

As the door closed, Walters, Strong, and Kit laughed out loud. A few seconds later, as the three men returned to their study of the report, there was a distant rumble, followed quickly by the shock wave of a tremendous explosion. Walters, Strong, and Kit and everyone in the room were thrown to the floor violently.

"By the craters of Luna," yelled Strong, "what was that?"

"One of the smaller screens has given way, sir!" yelled the chief electronics engineer after a quick glance at the giant control board. "Number seven."

Walters struggled to his feet. "Where is it?" he demanded.

Strong and Kit got to their feet and crowded around the commander as the engineer pointed out the section on the huge map hanging on the wall.

"Here it is, sir," he said. "Sector twelve."

"Has that area been evacuated yet?" asked Strong.

"I don't know, sir," replied the engineer. "Captain Howard

was in charge of all evacuation operations."

Walters spun around. "Get Howard, Steve. Find out if that part of the city has been cleared," he ordered and then turned to Kit. "You, Kit, take the Space Marines and round up every spare oxygen mask you can find and get it over to that section right away. I'll meet you *here*"—he placed his finger on the map—"with every jet car I can find. No telling how many people are still there and we have to get them out."

Almost immediately the wailing of emergency sirens could be heard spreading the alarm over the city. At the spaceport, where the citizens were waiting to be taken off the satellite, small groups began to charge toward the loading ships in a frenzy of fear. Since Titan had been colonized, there had never been a single occasion where the sirens had warned of the failure of the screens. There had been many tests, especially for the school-age children and the miners working far below the surface of the satellite, but this was the first time the sirens howled a real warning of danger and death.

Strong raced back to the control tower of the spaceport in a jet car and burst into the room where the captain was still asleep on the couch. Strong shook him violently.

"Wake up, Joe!" he cried. "Come on. Wake up."

"Uh—ahhh? What's the—?" Howard sat up and blinked his eyes. "Steve, what's going on?"

"The screen at sector twelve has collapsed. How many people are still in there?"

"Collapsed! Sector twelve?" Howard, still groggy with sleep, dumbly repeated what Strong had said.

Strong drew back his hand and slapped him across the face. "Come out of it, Joe!" he barked.

Howard reeled back and then sat up, fully awake.

"What—what did you say?" he stammered.

"Sector twelve has gone," Strong repeated. "How many people are left there?"

"We haven't even begun operations there yet," Howard replied grimly. "How long have I been asleep?"

"A couple of hours."

"Then there's still time."

"What do you mean?"

"Just before I folded, I ordered the evacuation crews to start working on sector eleven. They should be finished now and just about starting on twelve. If they have, we have a good chance of saving everyone."

"Let's go."

The two men raced out of the control tower to the jet car and roared through the desolate streets of the city. All around them commandeered jet cars raced toward the critical area. Commander Walters stood in the middle of an intersection on the main road to sector twelve, waving his arms and shouting orders to the enlisted guardsmen and volunteer miners that had raced back into the city to help. On the sidewalk, enlisted guardsmen handed out extra oxygen masks to the men who would search the area for anyone who might not have gotten out before the screen exploded. The main evacuation force that had been under Howard's supervision had already moved in but there was still a large area to cover.

"We'll split up into six sections!" roared Walters, standing on top of a jet car. "Go down every street and alley, and make a house-to-house search. Cover every square inch of the sector. If we lose one life, we will have failed. Move out!"

With Strong, Kit, Howard, Walters, and other officers of the Solar Guard in the lead, the grim lines of men separated into smaller groups and started their march through the deserted city. The swirling gas already was down to within a hundred feet of the street level. When it dropped to the surface, each man knew there would be little hope for anyone remaining alive without oxygen masks.

Every room of every house and building was searched, as over all, the deadly swirling gas dropped lower and lower and the pressure of the oxygen was dissipated.

Once, Strong broke open the door to a cheap rooming house and raced through it searching each room. He found no one, but something made him go back through the first-floor rooms again. Under a bed in a room at the end of the hall he found a young boy huddled with his dog, wide-eyed with fear. Such incidents were repeated over and over as the searchers came upon sleeping miners, sick mothers and children, elderly couples that were unable to move. Each time they were taken outside to a jet car where masks were strapped over their faces, and then driven to the spaceport. And, all the while, the deadly methane ammonia gas dropped lower and lower until it was within ten feet of the ground.

There were only a few buildings left to search now. The lines of the men had reached the open grassy areas surrounding the city proper, and as they collected in groups and exchanged information, Walters gathered them together.

"You've done a fine job, all of you," he said. "I don't think there's a living thing left in this entire sector. All volunteers and the first four squads of enlisted guardsmen and second detachment of Space Marines return to the spaceport and prepare to abandon Titan. Give all the aid to the officer in charge that you can. Again, I want to thank you for your help."

As the group of men broke up and began drifting away, Walters hurried over to Strong and Kit Barnard. "Steve," he said, "I want you to supervise the evacuation at the spaceport. Since this screen has blown up, those poor people are frightened out of their wits. And they have a right to be. If a major screen blew instead of a small one, we really would be in trouble."

"Very well, sir," replied Strong. "Come on, Kit, you might as well blast off with a load of children."

"Sure thing."

"Just a minute," Walters interrupted. "I would consider it a service, Kit, if you would send your young assistant back with your ship and you stick around until we get all the people safely off."

"Anything I can do to help, sir," replied Kit.

At that moment a tall enlisted spaceman walked up to Walters and saluted sharply. Walters noticed the stripes on his sleeve and his young-looking face. He couldn't remember ever seeing such a young master sergeant.

"Captain Howard asked me to make my report to you, sir," said the guardsman.

"Very well, sergeant," said Walters.

The young spaceman made a detailed report of his

search through sectors eleven and twelve. While he spoke, Strong kept looking at him, puzzled. When the guardsman had finished, Strong asked, "Don't I know you from somewhere, Sergeant?"

The guardsman smiled. "You sure do, Captain Strong. My name's Morgan, sir. I was a cadet with Tom Corbett and Astro, sir, but I washed out. So I joined the enlisted guard."

"Congratulations, Sergeant," said Walters. "You're the youngest top kick I've ever seen." He turned to Strong. "Apparently we slipped up, Steve, letting this chap get out of the Academy so he could make a name for himself in the enlisted ranks."

"Thank you, sir," replied Morgan, blushing with pride.

"Have you seen the cadets, by any chance, Sergeant?" asked Strong. "They're both here on Titan with me."

"Oh, yes, sir," said Morgan. "I saw them some time ago."

"Where?"

"A few blocks closer to the heart of town," said Morgan, pointing back down the avenue. "We were just starting in on sector eleven and I saw them coming out of a restaurant."

"Funny they haven't returned," commented Walters. "And what would they be doing down there?"

Strong's forehead creased into a frown of worry. "Sir, I wonder if you'd allow me a half hour or so to look for them?" he asked. "If they were anywhere near this section when the screen collapsed, they could have been injured by the sudden release of pressure."

"They had masks, sir," said Morgan. "I gave them a couple myself."

Walters thought a moment. "It's just possible they might have been injured in some way," he mused. "Go ahead, Steve. If you don't find them, and they don't show up at the spaceport, we'll organize a full search."

"Thank you, sir," said Strong. "You come along with me, Sergeant."

Adjusting their oxygen masks, Captain Strong and Sergeant Morgan strode down the street through the swirling mist of deadly methane ammonia to begin their search for Tom and Astro.

15

"LISTEN!"
**CAPTAIN STRONG GRABBED THE YOUNG MASTER
SERGEANT BY THE ARM AND STOOD STOCK-STILL**
in the swirling methane ammonia gas, his eyes searching
the misty sky.

"What is it, sir?" asked Morgan.

"A spaceship decelerating," said Strong, "coming in for a
touchdown!"

"I think I hear it now, sir!" said Morgan.

"Can you figure out where it is? I can't see a blasted
thing."

"Sounds to me as though it's to the left, sir."

"OK, let's go and investigate," said Strong. "There isn't
any good reason for a ship coming down in this deadly
soup—or in this area."

Walking slowly and cautiously, the two spacemen angled to the left, peering through the clouds of gas that
seemed to get thicker as they moved along. The roaring blast
of the ship became louder.

Strong put his hand out to stop Morgan. "Let's hold up
a minute, Sergeant," he said. "I don't want to get too close
until I know what we're facing."

They stood absolutely still, the gas swirling around them
in undulating clouds that grew thicker one minute and then
thinned out again. As the gas thinned for a few seconds,
Strong gasped and pointed.

"Look!" he cried. "By the craters of Luna, it's Brett's ship!"

"Brett?" asked Morgan.

"Charles Brett. He owns that ship. It's the one that won
the space race from Earth. Now, what would he be doing
landing out here?"

"I think he came down beside that warehouse up ahead, sir," said Morgan, as the gas cloud closed in again, cutting off their view of the actual landing. "It used to be a storehouse for mining gear a couple of years ago, but it's been empty for some time."

"I think we'd better check this, Sergeant," said Strong firmly. "Come on."

Strong started forward, then stopped, as a particularly heavy cloud of the deadly gas swirled around them. The two spacemen clung together blinded by the dense methane ammonia that would kill them in thirty seconds should their oxygen masks fail. In a moment the foggy death thinned out again and they continued toward the warehouse and the sleek black ship behind it.

TOM CORBETT AND ASTRO HEARD the roaring blast of the ship's exhaust. They saw Brett and Miles haul the instruments out of the cavern. They saw; they could hear; but they could not move. For nearly three hours they had remained alone in the cavern, frozen in the exact position they were in when Quent Miles had blasted them with his paralo-ray gun. And then Brett and Miles were standing before them again, Miles covering them with his paralo-ray gun.

"Why should we break our backs loading the ship?" sneered Miles. "Let them carry it out for us."

"All right, release them," agreed Brett. "But get that stuff loaded in a hurry. Walters is either getting suspicious or he's pulling a bluff. We can't take any more chances."

Miles flipped on the neutralizer switch of the paralo ray and leveled it at Tom. "We'll take the little fella first," he said. "If he acts up, we'll just leave the other fella the way he is."

He fired at Tom, and the young cadet began to shudder

violently. His teeth chattered and he found it difficult to focus his eyes as his nervous system tried to shake off the effects of the ray. He crumpled to a heap on the balcony floor and gasped for breath.

"He won't be much use to you for a while." Brett laughed. "Look at him flopping around like a fish out of water."

"Get up!" snarled Miles at Tom, quickly flipping the ray gun back to positive charge. "Come on. You're not that bad off. Get up." He leaned over and prodded the cadet with the gun. "If you don't get up, I'll freeze you again," he threatened.

Tom struggled to his feet. "I'll get you for this, Miles," he gasped weakly, his teeth still chattering.

"Never mind the hot air!" snarled Brett. "Go down there and start hauling up those boxes."

Tom turned helplessly and stumbled down the stairs to the floor of the cavern.

"Now for the big fellow," said Miles. He fired the neutralizer charge and Astro started to quiver at the shock of the release. But he clamped his teeth together and made a quick lunge for Miles, reaching for the spaceman's throat. Expecting the attack, Miles stepped aside quickly and brought the gun down sharply on the big cadet's head. Astro dropped to the floor, half-stunned. The black-clad spaceman leveled the ray gun and sneered, "Try that again, you overgrown punk, and I'll drop you on your head."

Astro shook his head and stumbled to his feet. He glared at Miles, spun away, and walked down the stairs shakily.

Miles and Brett stood on the balcony and watched the two cadets working on the cavern floor. "Hurry it up there!" shouted Miles. "We haven't got all day."

Brett took his ray gun from his belt and stepped forward. "I'll handle Corbett," he said. "You take care of the big one."

"Right," replied Miles. "But stay well in back of them and keep your gun on them all the time."

"How long do you think it'll take to get the ship loaded?" asked Brett.

"Couple of hours. But what are you going to do about Walters if he's wise?" Miles shrugged his shoulders.

"Simple," said Brett. "We take the stuff we've got, haul it

to the hideout, dump it, and return to Atom City. Then we just sit tight and wait until the situation clears up here on Titan."

"What about that investigation?" asked Miles, keeping his eyes on the cadets, who were now staggering back to the stairs, each carrying a heavy lead box containing the precious uranium pitchblende.

"What can an investigation prove?" snorted Brett.

"I don't know. Walters and Strong are pretty smart cookies."

"Unless they have witnesses that you were messing around Kit Barnard's ship, which they don't, and unless they find out about Ross, which they won't, there isn't anything they can do."

Miles looked down at the shorter man beside him. "Ross, eh?" He laughed.

Brett stared at him and then shrugged. "I always get mixed up," he said. "But you know what I mean."

"Sure, I know." Miles turned to watch Astro and Tom start up the stairs to the balcony, the lead boxes on their shoulders. "What are you going to do with them?" he said.

"Take them to the hideout and decide later. Besides, they'll be handy for unloading the ship."

"Good idea," nodded Miles. He took a deep breath and smiled. "I sure wish I could see Walters' face when he learns about the new load of uranium that'll flood the market."

Brett laughed. "Yeah, and with the customs clearance we'll get to haul in the crystal, there'll be no way they can figure out how it's getting in."

Miles turned and shouted at the two cadets struggling up the stairs. "Come on, you two. Get a move on."

"We're making it as fast as we can, Miles," Astro protested.

"It ain't fast enough," sneered the spaceman. He reached out with his free hand and slapped Astro across the mouth. "That's just to remind you to watch your tongue, or you might wind up an icicle again."

Astro dropped the box and crouched, his big frame ready to be released like a coiled spring. Miles backed up and fingered the trigger on the ray gun. "Come on, stupid," he snarled. "Come on, I'll give it to you again, only this time—" He smiled.

"No, Astro," called Tom. "There's nothing we can do now. No use getting frozen again."

"That's using your head, Corbett." Miles laughed. "Pick up that box and get going."

Astro picked up the lead box again and staggered after Tom toward the door. Miles and Brett stepped back, guns ready, and watched the two cadets walk slowly ahead of them into the tunnel.

CAPTAIN STRONG AND SERGEANT MORGAN crept to the side of the warehouse and flattened themselves against the wall. With the gas swirling around them thicker than ever, they found it more difficult than ever to see where they were going.

"I think I see a door ahead," said Strong.

"Want me to see if it'll open, sir?" asked Morgan.

"No. I'll look around in the warehouse," replied the Solar Guard captain. "You investigate the ship. If anyone's aboard, keep him there until I contact you. If not, come back here and wait for me."

"Very well, sir," said Morgan, and turned toward the black ship. In a moment he was lost in the deadly mist.

Strong made his way to the door and twisted the latch. The door slid open easily, and he stepped inside, closing it behind him and waiting for some signs of life or movement. The gas was like a thick fog in the room and he inched his way forward, hands outstretched like a blind person. Gradually he began to see the vague form of a door on the opposite wall and he made his way toward it, completely unaware that he came within inches of falling through the open trapdoor in the floor.

He opened the door in the wall slowly, peering inside cautiously. He was startled to feel the faint rush of air on his hands and to see the room clear of the dangerous methane ammonia gas. He moved quickly inside and made a hurried inspection of the gear, not bothering to look to examine it closely. He shrugged his shoulders. It was just as Morgan had said. An abandoned warehouse with old mining gear and nothing else.

Suddenly he stopped. There was something strange about the room and he looked around again. The gas! There were no ammonia vapors in the room. He quickly searched along the walls for some outlet of oxygen, remembering now the rush of air he had felt as he opened the door. Close to a corner near the door, he found a small opening. Air poured out of it in a steady rush. He straightened up, his face grim. "So that's it," he said to himself. "Somebody has been sucking off oxygen from the main pumps!"

Strong headed for the door. "But why?" he asked himself. "Why in this particular building?"

He strode out of the room and inched his way across the outer room toward the front door, again narrowly missing the open trapdoor.

Once outside, he made his way along the side of the building in the direction that Morgan had taken. When he reached the corner, he could see the black bulk of the *Space Knight* a hundred yards away. He ran toward the base of the ship and met Morgan coming toward him.

"Find anything, Sergeant?" he called.

"Nothing, sir," replied Morgan. "The ship is ready to blast off and her cargo holds are full. But that's all."

"Full of what?"

"I couldn't see, sir. The main hatch was locked and I could only see through the viewport. But it just looked like general cargo to me."

"Couldn't have been crystal?"

"It might have been, sir. It was pretty dark in the hold but it looked like a lot of boxes to me."

"You don't put crystal blocks in boxes," said Strong.

"Sometimes they do, sir. The more expensive grades are crated, so that the surfaces won't get scratched. Pieces that are going to be used for outer facings on a building, for instance."

"All right, Sergeant. But I found something back in that building that is going to prove very interesting."

"The cadets, sir?"

"No. An illegal use of oxygen!"

Quickly Strong explained his discovery, concluding, "Come on. We're going back in there for a closer inspection!"

"But we can't, sir," said Morgan.

"Why not?"

"We only have enough oxygen left in our tanks to get us back to the cleared area."

"Blast it!" growled Strong. "Aren't there any masks aboard the ship?"

"No, sir," replied Morgan.

"Very well, then. The only thing we can do is go back and bring out a searching party in force." Strong turned and walked rapidly away. "Come on, Sergeant, I think we're on the way to answering a lot of questions about the failure of the screens."

Almost running, the two spacemen disappeared into the swirling mist of deadly gases.

No sooner were they out of sight than Tom Corbett and Astro, faces covered with oxygen masks, emerged from the warehouse and headed toward the ship, Miles and Brett close behind them with paralo-ray guns leveled at their backs.

16 ROGER MANNING OPENED HIS EYES, THEN CLOSED THEM. HE LAY PERFECTLY STILL AND LISTENED.

The sound he heard was the unmistakable blasting roar of a spaceship. But there was another sound, much closer. In fact, it was in the room with him.

He opened one eye to see Quent Miles moving about in the one-room, airtight space hut which had been his jail for the last week. Miles was throwing clothes into a space bag, keeping a wary eye on Roger, sprawled on the bunk. Hoisting the bag to his shoulder, Miles closed the faceplate of his space helmet, turned to the airlock, and stepped inside, slamming the portal behind him. From the bunk, Roger could hear the hissing of the change of pressure inside the lock from normal to the vacuum of space outside.

The entire week had been a time of waiting and wondering. He couldn't understand Miles' actions in taking him prisoner the moment before blast-off from Earth, and then keeping him at the asteroid, seemingly giving up all chances of winning the race.

Roger waited until he was sure that the black-clad spaceman had gone, then he sat up and worked desperately on the thin metal chain binding his wrists. He had been working on one of the links ever since his arrival at Miles' strange asteroid base, scraping it against the rough metal edge of one of the legs of his bunk. Two days before, he had succeeded in wearing it down to a point where he could snap it easily when the opportunity came for him to make a break. But so far, the chance had not presented itself. He had been kept prisoner in the space hut, and Miles had pushed his food in through a vent in the airlock. Now, however, with the sound of the spaceship outside, the cadet decided it was time for action.

Working quickly, Roger snapped the link and tore off the chain, freeing his hands. He allowed himself the longed-for luxury of stretching just once, and then crossed to the small locker beside the airlock door to take out a space suit. He climbed into it hurriedly, secured the helmet, and began searching the small room for a weapon. In the bottom of a chest he found a rocketman's wrench. Grasping it tightly, he stepped into the airlock. Just before he turned on the oxygen in his space suit, he listened again for the noise of the blasting ship. Then he grinned as he realized that it wasn't the noise of the ship he heard, but the vibration it created on the surface of the asteroid. Sound wouldn't travel through the vacuum of space outside. Suddenly it stopped and Roger realized the tubes were being blasted in preparation for take-off. The young cadet closed the inner portal of the lock, adjusted the pressure, turned on the oxygen of his suit, and waited. In a moment the indicator showed the pressure to be equal to that outside in space, and he opened the outer portal cautiously.

A section of the asteroid belt swam above him. Hundreds of small planetoids and various-sized pieces of space junk drifted in the cold vacuum of space overhead. Roger looked around. The asteroid he was on was so small and the horizon such a short distance away that the base of Miles' giant black ship was half-covered by the curvature of the planetoid.

Holding the wrench tightly in his hand, the blond-haired cadet circled around the space hut cautiously, looking for Quent Miles, but the spaceman was nowhere in sight. He had walked all the way around the hut and back to the air-lock when he saw a movement out of the corner of his eye. It was Miles, returning to the space hut. Moving quickly, Roger ducked behind a huge boulder and waited for Miles to come closer. It would be impossible to hit Miles with the heavy wrench. The space helmet would ward off the blow. His only chance was to get aboard the ship while Miles was inside the hut. And he would have to move fast. When Miles discovered the hut was empty, he would come looking for the young cadet.

But to the cadet's great relief, Miles went past the hut and disappeared over the horizon of the asteroid in the op-posite direction.

Slipping out from behind the boulder and utilizing the near lack of gravity, Roger ran in giant leaps toward the black spaceship. His last jump brought him to the base of the ship where he quickly clambered up the ladder, opened the portal, and slipped into the airlock. In a matter of sec-onds he had built up the pressure in the lock to equal the pressure inside the ship. He opened the inner portal and raced up the ladder to the control deck. Throwing himself into the pilot's chair, he prepared to raise ship. Then he slumped in despair. The master switch had been removed. It was impossible for him to blast off!

He leaped out of the chair and scrambled up the ladder to the radar deck. He flipped on the audioceiver and nerv-ously waited for the tubes to warm up. Nothing happened. Only then he remembered that the communications would not work without power from the generators and they could not be started without the master switch.

"Boy! He sure wasn't taking any chances of me getting away and leaving him here," Roger muttered to himself, as he turned back to the ladder and climbed down to the airlock. He stepped inside, and crossing to the small viewport, looked out over the dead landscape of the tiny world for a sign of Quent Miles. He saw the black-clad spaceman returning toward the hut. Roger held his breath. If Miles went into the hut this time and found him missing, he would know that the cadet was aboard the ship. "Manning," Roger said to himself, "if you ever needed luck, you need it now!"

Miles walked slowly, as if in no hurry, still heading for the space hut. But as Roger held his breath in fear, he passed it again, without so much as pausing to look at it.

Roger grinned. "Spaceman, you are going to say your prayers every night after this," he murmured.

The cadet turned, and racing as fast as the cumbersome space suit would allow him, headed toward the power deck. Passing the galley, he snatched up several plastic packages of food.

Down on the power deck, Roger went directly to the lead baffling shields around the reactant chambers and carefully squeezed between them and the outer hull. It was going to be a rough ride on the power deck, jammed in behind the firing chambers, but at least he was hidden—and more important, *free.*

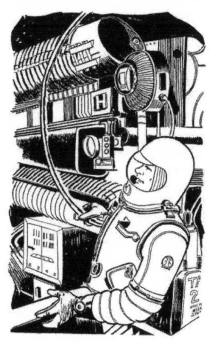

He listened for the clank of metal shoes on the ladder above him. When he heard them, followed closely by the slam of the airlock portal, he grinned in satisfaction. Opening one of the plastic bags, he began to eat.

In a moment the ship came to life and the power

deck became a raging torrent of noise and vibration. As Roger braced himself, he felt the ship quiver and then shake as, under heavy acceleration, it blasted off into space.

CAPTAIN STRONG AND YOUNG SERGEANT MORGAN hailed a passing jet truck loaded with Space Marines. "Get me to Commander Walters right away, Lieutenant!" said Strong to the young officer in charge. "This is an emergency."

"Yes, sir," acknowledged the young officer, and sent the truck roaring down the empty avenue toward the electronics building where Walters was still checking the reports on the screens.

"Is there anything new, sir?" asked the young officer. "Have the technicians been able to find out what's making the screens fail?"

"We're on the right track, Lieutenant," said Strong shortly. "Can't you get any more speed out of this thing?"

"Yes, sir," replied the officer. He rammed the accelerator to the floor and the small truck blasted through the streets as though shot out of cannon.

In a few minutes the truck screamed to a halt in front of the building and Strong leaped toward the door, followed closely by Sergeant Morgan and the Space Marine lieutenant.

Strong found Walters before the telemetering board waiting impatiently for some figures Dr. Joan Dale had sent him to be analyzed and evaluated. He spun around when Strong entered the room at a dead run.

"Steve!" he exclaimed. "What's the matter? Anything happen to the cadets?"

"We didn't find them, sir, but we did find something else. We—" Before Strong could finish, the calculator began pouring out its answers.

"Excuse me, Steve! These figures could tell us why the screens are failing."

"But I know why they're failing, sir!" shouted Strong.

"You know what?" exclaimed Walters.

As all the men in the room stared at him, Strong hurriedly told the commanding officer what he had found, concluding, "I think the room I stumbled into was used as a repair shop. But it was gas-free and pure oxygen was coming out of the pipe I described."

"I see," said Walters grimly. "Let me check that against these figures." He turned to the calculator and, with the assistance of Joe Howard, Kit Barnard, and the chief electronics engineer, began studying the figures.

Strong paced up and down nervously. The faces of the technicians in the room clearly showed the strain they had been under the past few days. And when they heard the startling news Strong had delivered, there wasn't one who didn't feel his fingers tighten into fists at Brett and Miles' selfishness.

Walters straightened up and glanced at the faces of the men around him. "Well, gentlemen," he said. "I think the figures speak for themselves."

There was a murmur of agreement. Walters turned back to Strong. "Those figures prove conclusively that what you say is true. It is impossible for the screens to collapse except from a vital leak—exactly such a leak as you have described."

Walters turned and began to snap orders to the men around him. "I want every available man sent out on the double. I want every inch of that area searched for an opening to a mine shaft or anything that leads underground. Take half the men off the spaceport detail."

"Shall we continue evacuation operations for the miners and their families?" asked the young Space Marine lieutenant. "There is quite a force of men out there that could be used in the search."

"What do you think, Steve? Should we take off the guardsmen and suspend evacuation in the hope that we can find that leak?"

"I would say yes, Commander," said Strong. "Your figures and those Dr. Dale sent you point to a leak of this nature."

"Very well, Lieutenant," said Walters. "Order every man to the area and begin search operations immediately. I want that leak found—and found fast! And I want Charles Brett and Quent Miles arrested at once!"

TOM AND ASTRO BENT OVER THE LEAD BOXES AGAIN and heaved them to their shoulders. A quick glance showed them that Miles had not followed them to the floor of the cavern as he had done before, but had remained on guard on the balcony.

As they struggled to lift the boxes to their shoulders, Tom whispered out of the side of his mouth, "I know how we can get out of here, Astro."

"How?"

"Since Brett is staying on the ship for this trip, Miles is going to have trouble watching both of us."

"Yeah, I know," muttered Astro. "Want me to jump him?"

"No," Tom growled. "Miles has been trailing us through the tunnel by twenty to thirty feet each trip. When we pass that spot where the light is, you drop your box. He'll be watching you then and that will give me a chance to grab that booby trap you took apart, remember?"

"Yeah!"

"OK. Now remember, when I give you the word, you drop your box on the right-hand side of the tunnel."

"Hurry up down there!" yelled Miles from the balcony. "We haven't got all night."

"Keep your shirt on, buster," growled Astro. "We're tired."

The two cadets balanced the heavy lead boxes on their shoulders, and, with Tom leading the way, climbed up the stairs past Miles and started up the tunnel in front of the black-suited spaceman.

They walked slowly, side by side, and as before, Miles stayed a good twenty paces behind them. As they neared the light where they knew the explosive charge would be, Tom began slowing his pace.

"Come on, get going, Corbett!" Miles yelled.

"He's tired," said Astro. "Leave him alone."

"What are you, his protector?" snarled Miles. "Get going, I said."

"OK," said Tom, struggling forward.

They came closer and closer to the light. Tom glanced at Astro and winked. Astro winked back and braced himself to fake the accident.

As closely as Tom could remember, Astro had tossed the charge to one side about ten feet beyond the light. If he knew exactly where it was, he could fall forward on top of it and stuff it in his tunic. He tried to recreate the scene as it happened. They passed under the light. One step ... two steps ...

three steps.... "Now, Astro," Tom whispered.

The big cadet lunged to one side, dropping the heavy box to the floor. At the same time, Tom dropped his box and lunged forward, arms outstretched, feeling along the floor for the precious explosives.

Miles ran up quickly, ray gun cocked and ready.

"Get up!" he shouted. "Get up or I'll freeze you both and leave you here!"

Tom and Astro struggled to their feet. They lifted the heavy boxes to their shoulders and started down the tunnel again.

When Astro dared a glance at Tom, he saw his unit mate grin and wink at him. Astro winked back. Suddenly it seemed that the heavy lead box was as light as air!

17 THE STREETS OF OLYMPIA ECHOED TO THE THUN-
DEROUS ROAR OF JET TRUCKS AND JET CARS RAC-
ING TO SECTOR TWELVE. Miners, Solar Guardsmen, and Space Marines jammed the vehicles, their faces grim with determination as they prepared for an all-out attempt to prevent the death of the colony.

Walters, Strong, and Kit Barnard sat behind Blake, the Space Marine lieutenant, and Sergeant Morgan as they rocketed through the streets. There was little conversation, each man thinking bitterly of Charles Brett and Quent Miles. Walters had already foreseen the possibility of trouble with emotional miners and had ordered Blake to be person-ally responsible for the safety of Miles and Brett when they were arrested.

"They get a fair trial like anyone else," declared Walters. "And they are innocent until proven guilty by a jury."

Now, as he sat beside Strong, Walters wondered if they would be able to save the city from the ammonia gas. He had taken a calculated risk in ordering guardsmen at the spaceport to aid in this search. If they should fail to find the leak, and the gas death spread farther across the city, the miners and their families would be helpless before it. The thought of the riots that would ensue if the people tried to get aboard the spaceships without order made the hardened commander shudder.

The jet car slowed and finally stopped. "What's the matter?" growled Walters.

"This is as far as we can go in the car, sir," replied Blake. "The gas is so thick I can't see where I'm driving."

"Very well. Put on your masks," Walters ordered. "Keep in contact with the spaceport control tower. They'll relay messages to me and my orders back to you. Let's go. Spaceman's luck."

The men opened the doors of the small jet car and stepped out into the swirling mists. Though there were more than a thousand men searching the area, they could not rid themselves of a strange feeling of loneliness as they each walked forward into the mists of death.

Strong and Walters inched their way down the street like blind men, feeling for each step with hesitant feet.

"Are you sure we're heading in the right direction, Steve?" asked Walters.

"Yes, Commander," replied Strong. "The warehouse is located about a half mile down this street."

"Of all the blasted messes," grumbled Walters. "We've got the finest radar system in the universe and we have to walk along here feeling our way like blind men."

"There's no other way, I'm afraid," said Strong grimly.

"Are you still with us, Kit?" called Walters.

"Right here, sir," came Barnard's voice, immediately behind them.

The spacemen continued their slow march through the mist in silence. Once, when Walters stumbled and nearly fell, he roared angrily.

"By the craters of Luna, when I get my hands on those two space crawlers, there won't be enough of them left for a trial!"

"Yes, sir," said Steve. "But if anything has happened to those cadets, you'll have to excuse ranks, sir, and wait your turn."

"Of course!" Walters exclaimed a moment later. "That's what happened to Manning! He didn't run away. He must have gotten on to them during the trip out here and they shut him up."

"Exactly what I was thinking, sir," said Strong, and then suddenly stopped. "I just bumped into a wall. We're here."

TOM AND ASTRO CLIMBED WEARILY through the trapdoor into the room above the main shaft while Quent Miles watched them closely, keeping his paralo-ray gun leveled. The two boys hitched the heavy lead boxes into a more comfortable position on their shoulders and started toward the door leading outside. But neither boy thought of his discomfort or weariness now. With the explosive charge safely hidden under Tom's tunic, they had a chance to fight back. It was a small chance, perhaps, but at least a chance.

Outside, they walked slowly through the swirling methane ammonia and Tom edged closer to his unit mate.

"Can you hear me, Astro?" he whispered through the mask amplifier. The big cadet simply nodded, keeping his eyes forward.

"We'll have to bluff our way now," continued Tom in a low whisper. "This stuff has to be set off with a charge of electricity."

"Where do we get it?" mumbled Astro.

"The paralo-ray gun."

"You're space happy. It won't work."

"I know that," hissed Tom. "But maybe Miles doesn't. I'll challenge Miles, hold the stuff right in front of me, and warn him that if he fires he'll set off the explosive and blow the four of us up."

"Oh, brother. That's a bluff to end all bluffs! Suppose he doesn't bite?"

"Then get set to take another paralo-ray charge."

"OK," sighed Astro. "When do you want to try it?"

"I'll give you the word," replied Tom. "Just be ready." The cadet turned away quickly. "Watch it," he hissed. "He's suspicious."

The two boys plodded along across the field as Miles moved up closer. He stared at them for a long moment and then continued to walk along directly behind them.

When they reached the ship, Miles allowed them to rest and catch their breath before making the long climb up the ladder to the airlock portal. Brett suddenly appeared in the open portal above them.

"Hey, Miles," he called, "is that the last of it?"

"Yes," Miles called back. "You get in touch with our pal?"

"Uh-huh. He's going to meet us out in space."

"In space?" Miles stared up at Brett with a strange gleam in his eye.

"Why not the hideout?"

"I don't know," Brett replied from above. "Let's not waste time talking now. Get those other two cases up here. I want to blast off."

Miles turned to the two cadets and waved his paralo-ray gun menacingly. "All right, you two. Get going!"

"Give us a few more minutes, Miles," said Tom. "We're so tired we can hardly move."

"Get up, I said," snarled the black-suited spaceman.

"I can't," whined Tom. "You'll have to give me a hand."

Miles pointed his gun straight at the young cadet. "All right. That means the big fella makes two trips and I freeze you right now."

"No, no!" cried Tom, jumping to his feet. "I can make it. Please don't freeze me again." Astro turned away to hide his smile.

Sneering his disgust at Tom's apparent fear, Miles prodded the cadets up the ladder. Tom went first, the heavy box digging into his shoulder. Astro followed, cursing the fog that prevented him from seeing where Miles stood below him so he could drop the heavy box on him.

Above them, Charles Brett watched them emerge out of the ammonia mist, ray gun held tightly in his hand. Tom climbed into the airlock safely and dropped the box on the edge of the platform, slumping to the deck beside it. Astro followed seconds later, and then Miles.

"Don't stop now," barked Miles. "Put those boxes below with the rest of them."

Tom got up slowly, leaning heavily on the outer edge of the precariously placed box. The box suddenly tilted and then slipped out of the airlock to disappear in the mist.

"Why, you clumsy—" Brett roared, raising his gun menacingly.

Astro stepped in front of Tom. "I'll get it," he cried. "Don't shoot!"

"Go on then," snarled Brett. "Go down with him, Miles. I'll stay here with Corbett."

"You go down with him," sneered Miles. "I've been up and down that ladder fifty times while you sat up here doing nothing."

"Is that so?" cried Brett angrily, turning to face the black-clad spaceman. This gave Tom the opportunity he was waiting for. He pulled the small charge of explosives from his tunic and held it in front of him.

"All right, you two!" he shouted. "Drop those paralo-ray guns. This is the booby trap you planted in the tunnel. You fire those ray guns and we all go up together."

Brett jumped back. Miles took a half step forward and stopped. "You haven't got the nerve," he sneered.

"Shoot and you'll find out," said Tom. "Go ahead! Shoot, if you've got the guts. Get down the ladder, Astro," he said. "They won't fire as long as I've got this in my hand."

Brett had begun to shake with fear but Miles brought his ray gun up slowly. He aimed it at Astro who was starting down the ladder, his head and shoulders still showing in the open airlock portal. Tom saw what Miles was going to do. "Jump, Astro!" he shouted.

Astro jumped at the exact instant Miles fired. "Rush him," cried Miles. Brett made a headlong dash for Tom, but the cadet sidestepped at the last moment and Brett fell headlong out of the ship, wailing in sudden terror as he fell to the ground.

Miles turned to Tom. He ripped off his mask and with his free hand closed the airlock portal.

"You fooled Brett, but you didn't fool me, Corbett." He laughed. "It takes a direct electric charge to set that stuff off. You just helped me get rid of a very obnoxious partner." He leveled his paralo-ray gun.

"I hate to do this," he said, "but it's you or me."

He fired. Tom was again frozen into that immobile state

more dead than alive. Miles laughed and hurried to the control deck.

ASTRO GOT UP ON HIS KNEES SLOWLY. Though the fall had been a hard one, he had rolled quickly with the first impact, thus preventing any injuries. He shook his head, regained his sense of direction, and then rose to his feet, starting back to the ship in hope of helping Tom. He tripped over something and fell to the ground. Groping around in the thickening ammonia gas he felt the still form of a body. For a moment, thinking it was Tom, his heart nearly stopped, and then he breathed a silent prayer of thankfulness when he recognized Charley Brett. He felt the man's heart. There was a faint beat.

Astro opened the valve on Brett's oxygen mask wide and waited until the man was breathing normally. Then he began feeling his way back to the ladder. Suddenly he heard a sound that made his blood run cold. It was the unmistakable whine of the cooling pumps building for blast-off. And he was directly underneath the exhaust tubes.

He scrambled away, heading back to the spot where  Brett lay. The whining of the pumps built to an agonizing scream. There were scant seconds left to save himself. He could not wait to find Brett. He began running wildly away from the ship, stumbling, falling, rising to his feet again to plunge on, away from the deadly white-hot exhaust blast of the *Space Knight*.

There was a terrific explosion, and then Astro was lifted off his feet and hurled through the mist, head over heels. He screamed and then blacked out.

"WE FOUND HIM ABOUT A THOUSAND YARDS AWAY from the warehouse, Commander," said the guardsman. "He looks pretty beat and his clothes are burned a little. I think he must have been caught in the blast of that ship we heard take off."

Walters looked down at Astro's big frame, sprawled on the ground, and then at the medical corpsman who was giving him a quick examination. The corpsman straightened up and turned to Walters and Captain Strong. "He'll be all right as soon as he wakes up."

"Shock?" asked Strong.

"Yes. And complete fatigue. Look at his hands and knees. He's been doing some pretty rough work." The corpsman indicated the big cadet's hands, skinned and swollen from his labor in the mines.

"Wake him up!" growled Walters.

"Wake him up!" exclaimed the corpsman. "Why, sir, I couldn't allow—"

"Wake him up. And that's an order!" insisted Walters.

"Very well, sir. But this will have to go into my report to the senior medical officer."

"And I'll commend you for insisting on proper care for your patients," Walters stated. "But in the meantime we've got to find out what happened. And Cadet Astro is the only one who can tell us."

The corpsman turned to his emergency kit. He took out a large hypodermic needle, filled with a clear fluid, and injected it into the big cadet's arm.

In less than a minute Astro was sitting up and telling Walters everything that had happened. When he told of the pipe that was sucking off the oxygen from the main pumps, Walters dispatched an emergency crew to the mine immediately to plug the leak. Then, when Astro revealed the secret of the mine, the presence of the uranium pitchblende, Walters shook his head slowly.

"Amazing!" he exclaimed. "Greed can ruin a man. He could have declared such a discovery and still had more money than he could have spent in a lifetime."

Walters spun around. "Steve, I want the *Polaris* ready to blast off within an hour. We're going after one of the dirtiest space rats that ever hit the deep!"

18 ROGER PEERED AROUND THE EDGE OF THE BAF-
FLING SHIELDS. The power deck was empty. He
edged out and stood upright, eyes moving constantly for signs of Miles.

No longer needing the cumbersome space suit, he
stripped it off and walked across the deck to the ladder. He
stopped to listen again but there was only the sound of the
rockets under emergency space drive. A quick glance at the
control panel told him that the ship was hurtling through
space at a fantastic speed. Satisfied that Miles was nowhere
near, Roger gripped the rocketman's wrench tightly and began climbing slowly and cautiously.

When he reached the next deck, he raised his head
through the hatch slowly. Then, in one quick movement, he
pulled himself up on the deck and ran for cover behind a
small locker to his right. Above him, through the open network of frames and girders, he could see the control deck,
but Miles was nowhere in sight.

Something on the opposite side of the ship caught his
eye. Miles' space suit hung on its rack, the heavy fishbowl-
like space helmet beside it in its open locker. Roger's heart
skipped a beat as he noticed the holster for a paralo-ray gun

nearby. But the large flap was closed and he could not see if it held a gun.

The young cadet moved away from the protection of the locker and started toward the space suit. He moved slowly, watching the upper deck where he figured Miles would be at the control board, operating the ship.

Suddenly Miles appeared above him, walking across the open control deck with a clip board in his hand, making a standard check of the many instruments. Before Roger could find a hiding place, Miles saw the cadet. He drew his paralo-ray gun quickly, firing with the speed of a practiced hand. Roger dove toward the space suit and wrenched open the holster but found it empty. Miles was behind him now, running down the ladder.

Roger spun around, darted to the ladder leading to the power deck, and just missed being hit by Miles' second shot. He jumped the ten feet to the power deck and darted behind the huge bank of atomic motors.

Miles came down the ladder slowly, gun leveled, eyes searching the deck. He stopped with his back to the rocket motors and called, "All right, Manning, come on out. If you come out without any trouble, I won't freeze you. I'll just tie you up again."

Roger was silent, gripping the wrench tightly and praying for a chance to strike. Miles still remained in one position, protected by the motor housing.

"I'm going to count five, Manning!" he shouted. "Then I'll hunt you down and freeze you solid."

Gripping the wrench tightly and raising it above his head, Roger eased out from his hiding place and slipped across the floor lightly. He was within four feet of Miles when the black-suited spaceman spun around and stepped back quickly. "Sucker," he snarled, and fired.

Roger stood motionless, his arm still raised, the wrench falling to the deck. Miles stuck his face close to Roger's head and said, "I don't know how you got here, but it doesn't make any difference now. In a little while you and your pal, Corbett, are going for a swim out in space."

Holding Roger by the arm, he tipped the boy over and lowered him to the deck. Roger's arm stuck up like the branch of a tree. Miles stood over him, flipped on the neutralizer charge of the gun, and fired again, releasing Roger from the paralyzing effect of the ray.

The young cadet began to shake violently and through his chattering teeth he muttered a space oath. Miles only grinned.

"Just wanted you to make yourself comfortable, Manning," he said. He flipped the gun to direct charge again and pointed it at the boy. Seeing it was useless to try and jump the burly spaceman, Roger relaxed and stretched out on the deck. Miles fired again calmly, and after testing the effect of the ray with his toe, he turned to the ladder.

As the spaceman climbed back to the control deck, Roger, though in a paralyzed state, could hear the communicator loudspeaker paging Miles.

"COME IN, QUENT! THIS IS ROSS! COME IN!"

Tom Corbett sat bound and gagged in the copilot's chair of the black ship, listening to Miles call again and again over the audioceiver. The fact that Miles was identifying himself as Ross puzzled the young cadet and he wondered if it was an alias. Tom was even more puzzled when Miles addressed the person he was calling as Quent.

"This is Ross! Acknowledge, Quent! Come in!"

Static spluttered over the loudspeaker and then a clear, harsh voice that was a perfect imitation, answered, "I read you, Ross," it said. "Where are you?"

Tom watched as Miles made a hasty check on the astrogation chart. "Space quadrant four," he replied. "Chart C for Charley! Where are you?"

"Same space quadrant, but on chart B for Baker," came the reply. "I think we can make visual contact on radar in above five minutes. Make the usual radar signal for identification. OK?"

"Good!" the *Space Knight* pilot replied. "What course are you on?"

There was a pause and then the voice answered, "South southwest. Speed, emergency maximum."

"Very well. I will adjust course to meet you. But what's the hurry?" asked Tom's captor.

"Better get out of space as soon as possible."

"Yeah, I guess you're right."

Tom listened intently. He closed his eyes and tried to visualize the charts and space quadrants he had heard mentioned. He knew the quadrants by heart, and knew that he was close to the asteroid belt. But each quadrant had at least a dozen or more charts, each one taking in a huge area of space.

"Is Brett with you?" asked the voice over the audioceiver.

"No. I'll tell you about it when we get together. All the rockets in space broke loose up there on Titan for a while."

"What do you mean? Hey! I think I just picked you up on my radar!" said the voice over the loudspeaker. "Give me the identification signal."

Tom watched Miles go to the radarscope and make a minute adjustment. The voice came over the loudspeaker again. "That's you, all right. Cut back to minimum speed and I'll maneuver to your space lock."

"Very well," replied the spaceman on the *Space Knight*.

He cut the rockets and in a matter of minutes the ship was bumped heavily as contact was made. The voice over the communicator announced the two space vessels had been coupled. "Open your airlock and come aboard."

"You come aboard my ship," said Miles. "We've got the stuff here."

"OK. But I have to go below and wake up that jerk, Manning."

"Wake him up?"

"Yeah. I got him frozen."

"All right, make it snappy."

Miles turned to look at Tom, a sneer on his face. "I'm giving you a break, Corbett," he said. "You're going to swim with your cadet buddy. You'll have company!"

Gagged, Tom could only glare his hatred at the black-suited spaceman. In a moment he heard the airlock open below and then footsteps clattered up the ladder to the control deck.

The hatch opened and Roger stumbled inside. He saw Tom immediately and yelled, "Tom! What are—" Suddenly he stopped. He looked at the man standing beside Tom and gasped in astonishment.

Tom watched the hatch as Roger's captor stepped inside. What he saw made him twist around in his chair and stare at the man beside him, utterly bewildered.

"Twins!" cried Roger. "Identical twins."

The man stepped through the hatch and walked over to his brother. They shook hands and slapped each other on the back.

"What happened to Charley, Ross?" asked Quent Miles.

"Just a minute, Quent," replied his brother. He turned and grinned at Tom and Roger. "Surprised, huh? Don't let it bother you. We've been driving people crazy ever since we were born. Does this tell you how we won the race?"

"T-t-twin pilots," stuttered Tom in amazement. "And twin ships?"

"Exactly." Ross laughed. "Pretty smart, eh?"

"Never mind them now," snarled Quent. "I've been sitting up there on that asteroid rock talking to myself. What happened to Charley?"

"Take it easy, will you, Quent?" said Ross. "I want to have some fun." He turned to Manning. "Untie Corbett and get on the other side of the deck. Have yourselves a nice long talk before you take your last walk."

Roger slowly bent over to untie Tom, muttering a space oath under his breath. The two brothers retired to the opposite side of the control deck and sat down. Ross kept his paralo-ray pistol in his hand and never once took his eyes off the two cadets.

"Well, what happened?" demanded Quent. "What are you doing here with Corbett and where in the blazes is Charley?"

"Charley is back on Titan, and probably dead," replied Ross easily. "He wouldn't pay any attention to us when we suggested plugging up the old tunnels when we started mining that uranium, so the oxygen which we were sucking off from the main screen supply took too much. The screens started to go. Practically the whole city is flooded with ammonia gas and it's being abandoned."

Roger and Tom stood quietly, listening, and when Roger heard the news he turned to Tom with a questioning look on his face. Tom merely nodded grimly.

"But what are you doing here with this load of pitch-blende?" Quent persisted.

"Everything would have been all right, even with the screens letting go," explained Ross, "if it hadn't been for Corbett and that big jerk Astro. They followed me out to the warehouse and down into the mine. Good thing we caught them, or we'd be on our way to a prison asteroid right now."

Quent glared over at Tom. "And Charley spilled the beans about the whole thing, eh?"

"Not exactly, but the Solar Guard knows enough to be suspicious," replied Ross. "We had some trouble with the radiation-detection gear and wanted to haul it out to the hideout for Manning to check. We decided to bring out as much of the stuff as we had mined, and when we caught Corbett and Astro snooping around, we made them load the ship. Corbett, here, got smart and Astro escaped. In the fight, Charley fell out of the ship. I don't know if he got away or not."

"Do we have a whole shipload of the stuff?" asked Quent.

Ross grinned. "About two million credits' worth."

Quent rubbed his hands together. "We're in clover." He laughed and slapped his brother on the back. "Well, I suppose the Solar Guard is looking for us by now?"

Ross grinned. "Right. So we pull the old trick, eh? We have two very likely prospects right there." He pointed to Roger and Tom.

"What is that supposed to mean?" snapped Roger.

"You'll find out, squirt," sneered Quent Miles.

"Wait a minute, Quent," said Ross. "I just thought of something. No one knows there are two of us, except these two punks here. We can't work the old gag. We can only use one of them."

"How do you mean?"

"Simple. The Solar Guard thinks Manning took it on the lam from Ganymede, right?"

Quent nodded.

"Well, we take Manning, dress him up in one of our outfits and stick him aboard the empty ship alongside. The ship blows up, and should they find anything of Manning, he'll be dressed like you, or me, and that will end the situation right there. Later, we can dump Corbett out in a space suit with a little oxygen, and write a note, sticking it in his glove. When they find him, they'll think he got away from Quent Miles, and when his oxygen gave out, wrote the note giving all the details. And who can say No, since Quent Miles, as such, will be dead?"

"End to the affair!" shouted Quent. "That's perfect."

The audioceiver behind them crackled into life, and there was a clear, piercing signal, a sign that an emergency transmission was taking over all channels. The signal continued until the clear, strong voice of Commander Walters flooded the control deck of the ship.

"Attention! Attention! This is Commander Walters of the Solar Guard! Attention all Solar Guard units in space quadrants one through seven—repeat, all ships in quadrants one through seven. This is emergency alert for the rocket ship *Space Knight*, believed to be heading for the asteroid belt. All ships are to institute an immediate search of quadrants one through seven for the *Space Knight* and arrest any and all persons aboard. Repeat. All ships...."

Ross Miles rose up and snapped off the audioceiver. "Come on. We've got to get out of here!"

"What about them?" asked Quent, pointing to Roger and Tom. "Will we have time to—?"

"Plenty of time," said Ross coldly. "Blast 'em now."

"With pleasure," replied Quent Miles, taking his gun from his holster.

"Jump, Roger!" shouted Tom.

Both boys threw themselves sideways as Miles leveled his gun.

Tom plunged headlong through the hatch door and scrambled down the ladder. Roger tried to follow, but Quent fired as Roger started to jump feet first through the hatch. His body became rigid as he tumbled through the hatch. Tom looked up just in time to break his unit mate's fall, but seeing that it would be useless to stay with him, left him on the deck and turned to flee through the depths of the black ship.

19 "NEVER MIND, MANNING!" SHOUTED QUENT MILES AS HE JUMPED PAST ROGER'S BODY. "We've got to find Corbett. Take the starboard ladder; I'll take the port. Search all the way aft to the exhaust tubes if you have to!"

Ross nodded quickly, hefted his ray gun, and moved down the opposite ladder.

Tom watched both of them come down like twin devils, hands holding the ray guns as steady as rocks. The cadet hid behind the open door leading to the lower cargo holds. Ross was the nearer of the two, walking like a cat, slowly, ready to spring or fire at the slightest movement. Tom quickly saw that if he jumped Ross, Quent would be on him in seconds. His only chance lay in their passing him, giving him the opportunity to return to the control deck and search for a ray gun for himself. And if that failed, at least he could call Commander Walters.

Ross crept closer. Tom crouched tensely. Should Ross see him, Tom would have to make an attempt to knock him out and get the ray gun before Quent could do anything.

"Careful, Quent!" called Ross as he moved toward the open hatch.

"You too," replied his brother. "This kid is plenty smart."

Tom breathed a silent prayer. Ross was now opposite the door. Should the black-suited spaceman decide to look behind it, Tom would be at his mercy.

Ross stopped beside the door and hesitated a moment.

"Hey, Ross!" Quent called, and Ross turned away from the door. "I think I hear something down inside the hold. Slip down the ladder a little way and cover me. I'll go down inside and look around. He must be down here somewhere, and if you guard the door, he can't get out."

Ross grinned. "Like flushing quail in Venus jungles," he said, moving away from the door and down into the hold where the lead boxes filled with uranium pitchblende were stored.

Tom could scarcely suppress a loud sigh of relief at his narrow escape. After a moment he peered cautiously around the edge of the door, and seeing the way clear to the control deck, ran back to the ladder. He paused at Roger's inert form and bent over, his lips close to the paralyzed cadet's ear.

"I'm going to try and find a ray gun," he whispered quickly. "If I can't, then I'm going to try and get in touch with Commander Walters or the Solar Guard patrols."

He patted the blond-haired cadet on the shoulder and raced up the ladder to the control deck. Once inside, he barred the door to the rest of the ship and began a frantic search of the many lockers and drawers. But it was fruitless. He could find no ray gun or weapon of any kind. Desperate, knowing that Ross and Quent would return to the control deck when they had searched the rest of the ship, Tom turned and scrambled up the ladder to the radar deck.

Again, barring the door behind him, he sat before the audioceiver and began calling the *Polaris*.

"This is Cadet Corbett aboard rocket ship *Space Knight* in quadrant four, chart C for Charley. Corbett aboard spaceship *Space Knight* in quadrant four, chart C for Charley! Come in, Commander Walters! Come in!"

Tom spun the dials on the audioceiver desperately, ranging over every circuit and repeating his cry. "This is Cadet Corbett! I am being held prisoner with Cadet Roger Manning aboard the spaceship *Space Knight* in space quadrant four, chart C for Charley...."

Suddenly the hum of the generators stopped and the glow of the tubes in the audioceiver died. Without a second's hesitation, Tom spun around and lunged for the door leading back to the control deck.

"They must have shut off the power," he decided. "When they didn't find me down below, they guessed that I came this way."

He raced through the control deck and down the ladder to the starboard companionway. If he could only get to the ship alongside!

He chided himself for not thinking of it before and darted toward the airlock that coupled the two ships together in space.

He turned a corner in the companionway and saw the door to the coupling chamber ahead. It was open. He dashed inside.

"Greetings, Corbett!" sneered Ross Miles. He stood just inside the doorway, the ray gun leveled at Tom.

"We figured you'd get around to thinking about the other ship sooner or later," said Quent behind him, jamming the ray gun in his back. "So we just came here and waited for you."

"Go get the other one, Quent," said Ross. Jerking Tom sideways into the coupling chamber, he rammed his gun into the curly-haired cadet's stomach. "I'll get this guy fixed aboard the other ship, and then set the firing chambers so they'll blow up."

"What are we going to do with Manning?" asked Quent.

"We'll figure that out later. Hurry up! Corbett probably called the Solar Guard."

"That's right, I did, Miles," said Tom. "They're probably closing in on you right now."

"Is that so?" snarled Quent. "Well, it's too bad you won't be alive to say hello to them."

"I WANT EVERY POUND OF THRUST YOU HAVE on that power deck, Astro," roared Commander Walters into the intercom. "We just received word from a freighter that picked up an SOS from Tom aboard the *Space Knight*."

Steve Strong and Kit Barnard sat in the pilot and copilot's chairs on the control deck of the *Polaris* and watched the needle of the accelerometer climb as Astro poured on the power in answer to Walters' command.

"If I know Astro," said Strong, "you'll probably get the fastest ride you've ever had short of hyperdrive, Kit."

Kit Barnard gulped as he watched the needle. "I see what you mean," he said.

Walters strode up and down the deck behind the two veteran spacemen, a scowl on his face. "By the stars," he rumbled, "this is the most incredible thing I've run up against in all my years in space!"

He paced up and down several times silently. "To think that two men could—*would*—jeopardize the safety and lives of thousands of people for—a—a uranium mine! It's beyond my comprehension."

"Excuse me, sir," said Sid, Kit Barnard's young assistant, coming down the radar-bridge ladder. "This report just came in from Titan spaceport control."

Walters took the message and read it quickly. He grunted and handed it to Strong. "They've found the mine and the leak," he said. "The screens are working again."

"Then you'll call off the evacuation operations, sir?" asked Strong.

"Right." Walters turned to Sid. "Son, send a message back to Titan control and tell Captain Howard to stop all evacuations as soon as he has enough oxygen to provide for the citizens of Titan. And then stand by for a general order to all units in this area."

"Yes, sir," said Sid, quickly climbing back up to the radar bridge.

The three men on the control deck fell silent as the ship hurtled through space. Each of them prayed silently for Tom and Roger's safety.

On the power deck below, Astro opened every valve and adjusted the firing chambers to their emergency maximum, forcing the giant ship faster and faster through space. And when he had done all he could, he paced up and down the deck, snapping a greasy wiping rag against his thigh again and again. His face showed the concern he felt for Tom and Roger, and at the same time, there was a questioning look in his eye. The auxiliary loudspeaker of the audioceiver overhead spluttered with static. He stopped to listen.

"This is Lieutenant Frazer aboard the Solar Guard cruiser *Hydra* to Commander Walters!" crackled an unfamiliar voice. "Come in, Commander Walters!"

Astro stared at the loudspeaker and held his breath.

"This is Walters on the *Polaris*. Go ahead, Frazer!"

"I am in command of a squadron of ships on space maneuvers in quadrant five, sir. Shall I abandon my orders and proceed under your general emergency alert to search quadrant four?"

"How many ships do you have with you, Lieutenant?" asked Walters.

"Three heavy cruisers and a rocket destroyer, sir," replied the voice across the gulf of space. "And I am fully armed, sir."

"Proceed to quadrant four, Lieutenant, and seize the vessel *Space Knight*." There was a pause, and then Astro's

blood ran cold as he heard the words, "and if necessary open fire!"

On the control deck, Captain Strong turned to Walters quickly. "But Tom and Roger, sir," he protested.

Commander Walters glared at Strong and turned back to the audio-ceiver. "Proceed to quadrant four," he said coldly. "Seize the vessel *Space Knight*, and if there is any resistance, open fire!"

"DID'JA HEAR THAT!" yelled Quent on the control deck of the *Space Knight*.

"I heard," replied Ross grimly. "With a whole squadron sweeping this quadrant we won't make it."

"What are we going to do?" asked Quent.

"We're staying right here."

"What?"

"Right here," said Ross. "Get Corbett off the other ship and set the fuses in the firing chambers to blow up after we cast off."

"But I don't see—"

"Don't ask questions!" snapped Ross. "Do as I tell you."

"OK." Quent spun away and headed for the coupling locks that held the two ships together. Ross turned back to the ladder and flipped his ray gun on neutralizing charge, releasing Roger from the effects of the paralo ray.

The blond-haired cadet staggered to his feet shakily. "Where's Tom?" he said, clenching his teeth to keep them from rattling. "If you've done anything to him—!"

"Take it easy, Manning," growled Ross. "Just get up on the control deck and behave."

Roger glared at the spaceman, and realizing it would be useless to jump him in his weakened condition, started up the ladder. Ross followed at a careful distance.

A few minutes later Quent appeared on the control deck, forcing Tom ahead of him. "All right," he growled. "What do I do now?"

"Did you cast off the other ship?" asked Ross. And when Quent nodded, he jerked his head toward Tom and Roger and barked, "Cover them!"

As Quent stood before the two cadets, his gun leveled, Ross strode to the audioceiver and flipped it on. "This is Quent Miles to Commander Walters aboard the *Polaris*," he called. "Come in, Walters."

Tom and Roger looked at each other, puzzled.

"If you can hear me, Walters, this is Quent Miles. I'm surrendering to you. And you alone! Call off your squadrons and come alongside in the *Polaris* by yourself. If you hear me, Walters, you better do what I say, or you'll never see Manning and Corbett again." He flipped the audioceiver off and grinned at his brother. "When Walters comes aboard, he's going to get a nice surprise."

"Like what?" demanded Tom.

Ross grinned wickedly, looking very much like the devil incarnate. "You heard Walters' order to open fire, didn't you?" he said. "It seems that Space Cadets aren't worth much as hostages. But what do you think it will be like with a full-fledged commander in our hands, eh? And a rocket cruiser like the *Polaris* to run around in."

"You wouldn't dare kidnap Commander Walters!" exclaimed Tom.

"Oh, no?" Ross laughed. "Listen, punk, with a murder charge hanging over our heads, and a couple of million credits' worth of pitchblende in the holds, both of us would do anything! And don't you forget it!" He turned to his brother. "Come on over here, Quent, and I'll tell you what we're going to do."

When the two spacemen were out of earshot, Tom turned to Roger. "How do you feel, Roger?"

"As if I'm going to shake myself apart," replied the radar-deck cadet, his teeth still chattering from the effects of the paralo ray.

"Well, hold on just a little bit longer, boy, because the next few minutes might spell the difference between getting out of here and—"

Tom was cut off by a sudden blast from the loudspeaker of the audioceiver.

"This is Commander Walters!" came a clear voice. "I accept your proposal, Miles. But I warn you, if anything has happened to those boys—"

"No, Commander!" yelled Tom. "It's a trap!"

"...You will suffer for it," the voice continued.

"No use, Tom," said Roger. "The set was only on reception."

The two boys looked at each other and then across the control deck to the grinning faces of the twins, Quent and Ross Miles.

2 0 "EASE HER UP A LITTLE MORE, STEVE!" COMMANDER WALTERS STOOD AT THE VIEWPORT watching the mighty *Polaris* slide alongside the black ship toward the coupling devices that would lock the two ships together in space.

"A little more!" said Walters. "About twenty feet!"

"Short burst on the main jets!" Strong called into the intercom.

"Aye, aye!" shouted Astro from below.

The giant ship inched along, the skins of the two ships barely touching.

"That's it!" shouted Walters. "The magnetic coupling links are in place. We're locked together!" He turned to Strong and Barnard. "Secure ship and come with me."

"Are you going to leave anyone on the ship, sir?" asked Strong as he cut all power.

"No, I want everyone with me," replied Walters. "No telling what Miles might try. As soon as we get aboard, spread out and search the ship. Find Tom and Roger if you can and then come up to the control deck."

"Aye, aye, sir," acknowledged Strong.

Walters turned to the audioceiver and spoke sharply into the microphone. "This is Walters, Miles. We're alongside and preparing to board your ship. I warn you not to try any tricks. I've accepted your surrender and hold you to it on your honor as a spaceman!" He paused, waiting for acknowledgment, then called again. "Are you there, Miles?"

There was a crackle of static over the loudspeaker and Miles' voice rang out on the control deck of the *Polaris*. "I'm here, Walters. Come on aboard!"

Walters turned to Strong and Kit. "Let's go. You know your jobs, so search the ship and report on the control deck." He strode toward the coupling locks that held the two ships together in space.

Aboard the black ship, Quent and Ross Miles smiled at each other. "You know what to do, Quent?" said Ross.

The brother nodded. "All set!" he said.

"Get going then. And don't make a move until you hear me draw their attention!"

"Right!"

The two brothers shook hands and Quent turned away, hurriedly leaving the control deck. Ross walked over to Tom and Roger, who watched the scene with anxious eyes.

"I really hate to do this, boys," he said, "but as you can see, things are pretty tight!" With that, he suddenly brought the butt of his ray gun down hard on Roger's head. The blond-haired cadet slumped to the floor. Tom leaped at the spaceman, but before he could close with him, Ross stepped back quickly and brought the gun down sharply on his head. The cadet slumped to the deck.

Quickly Ross propped them up against the bulkhead.

Then, after a fast look around the control deck for any last thing he might have forgotten, he walked casually over to the control station and sat down. Seconds later Walters and Strong stepped inside.

"I arrest you for murder, willful destruction of Solar Guard property, and illegal operation of a uranium mine, Quent Miles!" said Walters. The spaceman shrugged and said nothing.

Strong bent over the unconscious forms of the two cadets and tried to bring them to, but they failed to respond.

"Better leave them alone, Steve," said Walters. "We have to get a medical officer for them. They look as if they've been bumped pretty hard."

Strong stood up abruptly and walked over to Miles, who lounged casually in his chair. Ignoring Walters, the Solar Guard captain stood in front of the black-suited spaceman, his jaw within an inch of the other man's face.

"If anything serious has happened to those two boys, Miles," he said in a cold, flat voice, full of menace, "I'll tear you apart!"

Miles paled for an instant and then grinned uneasily. "Don't worry about it, Strong. They're pretty tough kids."

Kit Barnard suddenly burst into the control room. "I've searched the cargo holds, Commander," he said. "Nothing there but lead boxes. Didn't find the boys—" Barnard stopped suddenly at the sight of the two unconscious cadets. "Tom! Roger!" he cried.

"They were slugged, Kit," said Strong. "You go back to the *Polaris* and send out an emergency call. Find the closest ship with a medical officer aboard and arrange for a meeting out here in space. We'll be ready to blast in five minutes."

"OK, Steve," replied Kit, turning to the door and then stopping to glare at Miles. "And save a piece of that space rat for me!"

Under Barnard's steely look, Miles rose to his feet and stepped back hesitantly. Then, suddenly, he jumped up on the chair, scrambled to the top of the master control panel, and crouched there tensely.

Strong, Walters, and Kit were momentarily stunned by his strange action. It seemed like a senseless and futile effort to get away. There was no way Miles could get out of the control deck or off the ship.

Beyond the reach of anyone on the control deck, Miles began to laugh.

Walters turned beet red with anger. "This is stupid, Miles!" he roared. "You can't get away and you know it!"

"That all depends on where you're standing, Walters!" said a voice from the hatch.

The three spacemen whirled at the sound of the voice and were dumfounded by the appearance of Quent Miles, standing to one side of the hatch, holding an automatic paralo-ray rifle, trained on them.

"Stay right where you are," he said softly. "The first man that moves gets frozen solid!"

Walters, Strong, and Kit were too stunned to make a move. They could only stare in open disbelief at Quent Miles.

"Come on down, Ross!" called Quent. "And if anyone tries to stop him, I'll let all three of you have it!"

Ross climbed down from the control panel and stripped the three helpless spacemen of their weapons. He threw them out of the hatch and then went to stand by his brother. As they stood side by side, Strong and Walters couldn't help but gasp at the identical features of the two men.

"You can never hope to get away, either of you," growled Walters, when he finally regained his composure.

Quent laughed. "We're doing more than just hope, Walters."

"Just for your information," Ross chimed in, "we're changing ships and taking the cargo with us." He backed toward the hatch slowly. "Come on, Quent." The two brothers stepped back through the doorway, Ross keeping his rifle leveled at the three men.

Safely outside, Quent slammed the heavy door closed. Then, with a rocket wrench, he worked on the outer nuts of the door used in emergency to seal off the ship by compartments.

"All set!" said Quent, stepping back. "They can't get out now until someone comes and loosens up those nuts."

"Get down below and start transferring that cargo to the

Polaris," ordered Ross, slinging the rifle over his shoulder. "I'll get on the audioceiver and tell that cruiser squadron to go back."

Quent laughed. "You know, Ross, this is terrific," he chortled. "We not only get away, but we get ourselves a Solar Guard rocket cruiser. Nobody'll be able to touch us in that ship."

"Nobody but me, Miles!" said a voice behind them. The two brothers spun around to see Astro, stripped to the waist, a heavy lug wrench in his hand, legs spread apart, ready to spring.

"Had me fooled there for a while, Ross!" he growled. "I saw your brother back at the Academy and thought it was you. But he didn't have the split ear lobe, the one I gave you. Remember?"

Ross slowly reached for the rifle that was slung over his shoulder.

"Don't do it, Ross!" warned Astro. "Get your hands off that rifle or I'll ram this wrench down your throat!"

Ross lowered his hand again slowly.

"Who is this guy, Ross?" asked Quent, licking his lips nervously. "How does he know about us?"

Ross kept his eyes on Astro, glaring at the cadet in hot fury. "I met him on a deep spacer, five years ago, when you were laid up in the hospital," he said between his teeth. "This punk was a wiper on the power deck. I was his petty officer."

"We got into a fight," snarled Astro, "when he wanted to send me into a firing chamber without letting it cool off first."

"There are two of us now, Astro!" said Ross.

Astro nodded slowly. "That's right. Two of you!" Suddenly he dove toward the two men, arms outstretched. With one mighty swipe of the wrench he knocked Quent unconscious. Ross was hurled against the bulkhead by the impact but managed to stay on his feet. Desperately he tore the paralo-ray rifle from his shoulder, but before he could level it, Astro was upon him, wrenching it out of his grasp. Pushing Ross away, he calmly broke it in two and threw the pieces to one side. Then he faced the black-clad spaceman squarely.

"I was a kid when I first saw you, Ross," he said between his teeth. "So you had me fooled like everyone else. When your brother showed up at the Academy with his ears in good shape, I thought it was a curious coincidence two guys should look so much alike. And on Titan, when you had me hauling up those boxes, you wore your hat all the time, along with the oxygen mask, so I didn't think anything of it. But now I know!"

All the while Astro talked, the two men circled each other like two wrestlers, each waiting for his opponent to make a mistake.

"So you know!" sneered Ross. "All right, wiper, come on!"

The black-suited spaceman suddenly dove straight at Astro and the cadet caught the full force of his body in his stomach. He sprawled on the deck, gasping. Miles was on top of him in a second, hands at Astro's throat.

Fire danced in the cadet's brain as Ross Miles' steely fingers closed around his windpipe. Slowly, with every ounce of strength he had in his body, Astro grasped Miles' wrists in his hands and began squeezing. The fingers around the muscular wrists were the fingers of a boy filled with hate and revenge. Slowly, very slowly, as the seconds ticked away and the 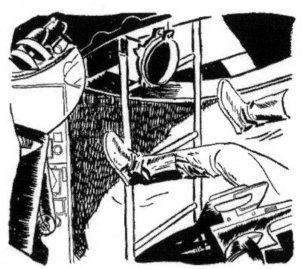 wind whistled raggedly in his throat, Astro increased the enormous pressure.

Now he felt the fingers around his throat begin to relax a little, and then a little more, and he kept tightening the pressure of his mighty hands. Expressions of surprise and then pain spread across Miles' face and he finally relaxed his grip around Astro's throat. He struggled to free himself from the viselike grip but it was hopeless.

Astro continued to apply pressure. He forced Miles up from his chest and then up on his feet, never relenting. Miles' face was now twisted in agony.

They stood on the deck, face to face, for almost a minute in silent struggle. There seemed to be no end to the power in the cadet's hands.

Suddenly Ross Miles slumped to his knees and sprawled on the deck as Astro let him go. The black-clad spaceman had fainted.

"THEY GOT A COUPLE OF HARD BUMPS, but they'll be all right," announced the medical officer, straightening up. "But that man outside, Ross Miles, is going to stand trial with a broken wrist!" He turned to Strong. "What do you feed these cadets?"

Strong smiled and replied, "These are special types we train to take care of space rats!"

Tom and Roger lay stretched out on emergency cots set up on the control deck of the *Polaris*. They grinned weakly at Astro, who hovered over them solicitously.

"This is the first time we've ever wound up an assignment on our backs, you big Venusian hick!" said Roger. "And I suppose I'll have to thank you for saving my life!"

Astro grinned. "Wasn't much to save, Roger."

"Listen you!" Roger rose on one elbow, but the medical officer pressed him gently back on the cot.

"Did you ever find out how Bill Sticoon's ship was sabotaged, Captain Strong?" asked Tom.

"We sure did, Tom," said Strong. "One of Brett's confederates slugged the Solar Guard officer in charge of monitoring the race on Deimos and took his place. If it hadn't been for a brash stereo reporter that kept taking pictures of everything and everyone, the impersonator wouldn't have been caught."

"And to think that I wanted to give that reporter a few lumps!" Tom exclaimed.

"Did you find out anything about the crash of Gigi Duarte's ship, sir?" asked Roger.

"Yes. Ross confessed that he was in Luna City and planted a time bomb on Gigi's ship when the *French Chicken* came in for refueling."

"Say," exclaimed Roger, "I just happened to think! With Miles disqualified, Kit wins the race!"

Seated in the pilot's chair, Kit turned to Roger and waved a paper. "Here's the contract, Roger. Signed, sealed, and with only the crystal to be delivered."

"There's only one thing bothering me now," sighed Tom.

"What's that, Tom?" asked Strong.

"Do you think I could get a three-day pass before we go back to class at the Academy?"

Strong and Kit looked at each other, puzzled. "With sick leave, you'll have plenty of time," said Strong. "Why a three-day pass especially?"

Tom settled deeper into the cot. "Well, sir," he said, grinning, "I figure it'll take just about three days for Astro and Roger to argue it out about who did the most to catch Ross and Quent Miles. **AND I DON'T WANT TO HAVE TO LISTEN TO IT!**"

★ ★ ★ ★ ★

TOM CORBETT AND HIS PALS
WILL RETURN IN
SABOTAGE IN SPACE

TOM CORBETT ★ ★ ★ ★ ★

SPACE CADET:

THE REVOLT ON
VENUS

CAREY ROCKWELL

TECHNICAL ADVISOR: WILLY LEY

ENJOY EXCITING SCIENCE FICTION ADVENTURES IN EVERY ISSUE OF BLACK INFINITY MAGAZINE.

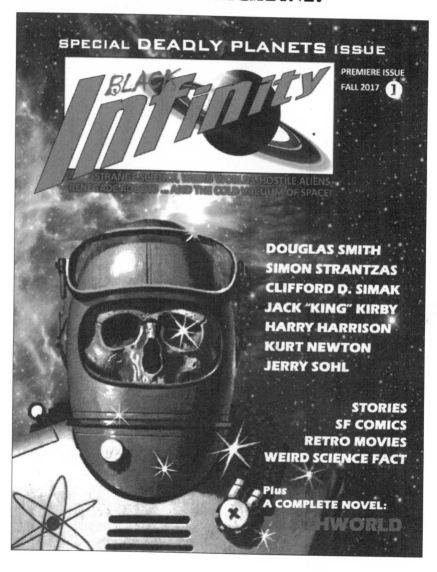

You might also enjoy:

DIET FOR DREAMERS:
Inspiration to Feed Your Dreams, Encouragement to Foster Your Creativity   ISBN: 978-0-9796335-7-7

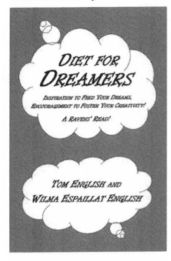

Five dozen witty and inspiring articles highlighting everything from Sherlock Holmes to Slinky toys, Stan Lee to Lucille Ball, the Monkees to Mother's Day, Hershey's chocolate to Julia Child, and much much more; plus, handling fear, rejection and failure.

Everyone has a special dream. Whether you're an artist or a writer, an actor or a singer, an inventor or an entrepreneur; or simply someone who dreams of better days ahead, Tom and Wilma English want to help you achieve your goals, by encouraging you to faithfully pursue your dreams while providing you with practical advice and inspiring stories. In this collection you'll discover fascinating facts and a few humorous turns about men and women, young and old, who dreamed big and succeeded despite shaky circumstances, overwhelming obstacles and, often, the silly notions of our wonderful, whacky world.   **$7.95**

Made in the USA
Middletown, DE
23 November 2018